UFO DOWN

A SCI-FI MYSTERY NOVEL

DC ALDEN

"Two possibilities exist. Either we are alone in the universe or we are not. Both are equally terrifying."

'*STEADY. STEADY. HOLD THAT...BOMBS GONE!*'
Arty Fraser's voice crackled through Harry Wakefield's headphones, and a moment later he felt the Lancaster bomber soar higher into the freezing night sky as six tons of explosive payload dropped out of the belly of the aircraft and whistled down to the target area below.

Harry powered his clear perspex dome in a quick circle, sweeping the surrounding blackness with the muzzles of his Browning .303 machine guns. Far below, white flashes lit up the rail yards as thousand-pound bombs obliterated rolling stock and tore up train tracks.

'*Photograph taken, skipper.*'

The Lancaster rattled violently as Captain Jonny Marsh banked the aircraft around and gunned the engines. Now it was all about getting home fast, and in one piece.

'Jesus!'

Harry ducked as a fleeing Lancaster thundered overhead, a giant black shadow only twenty feet above his top turret. *That was close.* Getting shot down was one thing; colliding with a friendly was a pointless death. After forty-seven combat missions over Fortress Europe, during which Harry, his crew-mates and *Margot*—the nickname for their beloved aircraft—hadn't suffered so much as a scratch. The twenty-two-year-old from Ilkeston in Derbyshire knew they were all riding their luck. So many friends and comrades had died, yet here they were, still breathing, still in one piece. Still fighting. Harry wasn't much of a churchgoer, so if it wasn't God watching over him, it had to be someone else. Lady Luck, perhaps.

Maybe it was She who'd helped them survive mission after mission into the black heart of Nazi Germany, to dodge the often impenetrable clouds of flak, to avoid the vengeful night-fighters and their superior radar, not to mention mechanical failure, pilot error, or a host of other mishaps that, in wartime, often made the difference between returning home or never seeing it again. Yet there was hope for all of them. The war had been costly, both in men and aircraft, but the Nazis were finally on the back foot. Jerry was getting squeezed on both fronts. With any luck, the war would be over by Christmas.

He heard Marsh's voice over the intercom.

'Keep your eyes open, chaps.'

'Roger, Skipper.'

Harry spun his turret around, watching the sky. On the plus side, the night was moonless, the burning rail yards to the south and east the only visible light in any direction. The darkness was their friend, and now they were travelling fast and light. Apart from the threat of night-fighters, the only other problem now was the weather.

The wind, in fact. The flight over from England was as bumpy as Harry could remember, and the icy northerly wind that carried snow all the way down from the arctic circle and dumped it across Europe was now trying its best to blow them off course. Or worse, into each other. Harry could feel *Margot* repeatedly banking to the north to stay on course. It wasn't long before they gave the order, and Marsh confirmed it—*breaking formation*. Harry watched the Lancaster above them slip to the south and disappear into the void.

Margot shook as Marsh coaxed her towards her maximum operating ceiling of twenty-one-thousand feet. Harry pedalled the turret left and right, his Brownings cocked and ready. Soon they were alone, the earth a pale blanket far beneath them, the sky a cold, lifeless void.

Harry flexed his fingers to keep them warm. He grabbed a rag from the recess beneath his seat and gave the Perspex turret a wipe. Looking down the fuselage he saw Joe Pyle, *Margot's* tail-gunner, swivelling left and right, but there was nothing to the east or south of them. Even the rail yard fires had disappeared over the horizon.

'*Cloud bank coming in from the north,*' Marsh's voice crackled over the intercom. '*We're going to duck in there for a bit, try and stay out of trouble.*'

The turret whined as Harry swivelled it around to face north. The cloud bank was enormous, pale against the night sky and towering up to the heavens. Bumpy it might be but it would serve them well if they could ride it all the way back to Norfolk. Wisps of grey cloud became clumps, and moments later they were thundering through the sky, invisible.

Harry felt himself relax a little. It wasn't complacency—they were all too experienced for that—but if a Jerry fighter wanted to find them he'd practically have to run into them. So, a respite then. Small, but welcome. He smiled as he thought about the navigator, Spencer, sweating over his charts and compasses. With no visual landmarks, Spence would have to work for his supper this evening, but he was one of the best. He would get them home.

'*Got something on our tail. Directly behind us.*'

Harry spun his turret around, his gloves gripping the handles of his Browning machine guns, his eyes searching the sky behind *Margot's* tail.

'*What've you got, rear-gunner?*'

'*Not sure, Skip. Thought I saw a light through the cloud. Below us, due east.*'

Harry could see Joe's turret moving, the clouds whipping across the fuselage between them. *Margot's* engines droned.

'*Talk to me, rear-gunner.*'

'*Sorry Skip. I thought I—Jesus Christ! There! Coming up beneath the starboard wing! Look at that thing move!*'

Harry swung the turret around, his fingers hooked inside the trigger guards of his Brownings —

Then he froze. A strange green light reflected off the clouds, off *Margot's* fuselage, and then Harry saw it, an airship, but one he'd never seen before, flying a dozen yards off the starboard wing. It was huge, three, maybe four times the size of *Margot*, its black fuselage smooth and shiny and seemingly devoid of rivets and seams. There was no cabin beneath it, no lights, other than a soft green glow coming from an exhaust port at its tail. Harry had seen nothing like it in his life.

'*Are you chaps seeing this?*' Marsh asked from the cockpit. Everyone responded affirmatively.

'*It's not an airship. Too fast. No engines, either.*'

'*Can't see any cockpit or cabin. What the hell is it?*'

'It's amazing,' Harry gasped. He panted like a dog inside his oxygen mask. 'Can't hear any engine noise either. Something that close, we should be able to hear it.'

'*Foo fighter,*' Arty Fraser's voice hissed. '*We've all heard the stories, right?*'

'*Recommend we put a little distance between us, skipper. That thing's lighting us up.*' It was Spencer, his voice calm, reasoned. Spencer never flapped.

'*If it was Jerry he would have opened up on us by now,*' Joe said from the rear turret. His voice wasn't calm, but it was a long way from panic. He sounded like he was in awe of it. And Joe was right; it wasn't the enemy. Harry had an unmistakable feeling that whatever its reason for being there, its intentions were friendly. Playful, even. Harry swung the turret around as the object slipped effortlessly beneath *Margot* and came up on the port wing. It sped up ahead of them, silently, then held its position, cloaked in that strange green glow that reflected off the clouds like a giant firefly. Guiding them, Harry sensed. Was that its intention? Was it leading them to safety?

The tracer rounds zipped past Harry's turret, angry red bees buzzing through the cloud. *Margot* shook as several of them punched their way through her fuselage in showers of sparks. Incendiary rounds. Harry knew it then; forty-seven missions and the biggest thing to hit them in all that time was a flock of seabirds over the Belgian coast. Despite their better judgement, they'd felt invincible. They were so close to the finish, but Harry knew it was not to be. Lady Luck, or whoever had kept them alive for so long, had finally abandoned them.

Harry heard the whine of the fighter jet as it shot past somewhere in the darkness. As the noise of its engine faded, Harry turned towards the nose of the aircraft where the green glow still reflected off the clouds. As he watched, the object sped away and vanished in an instant.

He heard Joe's Brownings open up, saw his outgoing

tracer lancing through the clouds. Harry fired too, tracking his own rounds parallel to Joe's, hoping the Jerry pilot would fly into them unwittingly. The Brownings shook in his hands. Brass rattled at his feet. The whine of the hydraulic turret competed with the roar of *Margot's* engines as the skipper put her nose into a shallow dive. That's when Harry saw them coming, knew they would make impact. When they did the sound was terrifying, the glowing rounds punching through *Margot's* thin skin, through Arty's flesh and bone, his awful scream, Spence's quiet encouragement to get us the hell out of here.

Harry glimpsed the fighter as it sliced through the cloud behind them and levelled out. A Messerschmitt 110, fast and deadly. Harry and the Kraut fired simultaneously, Harry's rounds tumbling through the night sky, the incoming rounds chewing up Joe in his rear turret, shredding *Margot's* tailplane. The 110 banked away into the cloud. *Margot* shuddered from nose to shattered tail. Smoke filled Harry's turret. He was blind.

He cranked the vent, and the smoke cleared, long enough for him to see the port engines belching flame that enveloped the wing. Smoke caught in Harry's lungs. He coughed violently. He heard the roar of the Messerschmitt and felt more rounds punching through *Margot's* body. The old girl was dying. Marsh knew it too.

'Bail out! Everyone, bail out now while I keep her steady!'

Harry felt his backside warming up. His parachute was in a compartment below his turret because it was too bulky to wear in the gunner's seat. He reached down, but the heat made him pull his hands back. Through the smoke below him, everything was on fire.

Including Harry's parachute.

The smoked thickened. His lungs screamed. *Margot* screamed too and started to pitch steeply, nose first. The Skipper must've got out, hopefully the others too. Harry prayed they did, because he wasn't going to make it.

He knew men who'd survived fire, who still lay in hospital, the horribly charred and disfigured husks he'd once called friends. Harry promised himself he'd never go out like that. If he was going to die, it would be on his terms.

The flames engulfed his parachute. Harry uncoupled his oxygen and heated suit and dropped into the main cabin. Then he stumbled through the flames towards the rear door. It was already open, and Harry felt a moment of relief—someone had made it out.

Margot groaned again, not in pain this time but with a fatal acceptance. Her nose pitched steeper. Harry had seconds to act. There was no time to find another parachute. As *Margot* spiralled out of the sky, flames engulfed Harry. He threw himself out into the night sky.

The wind extinguished the flames, but it didn't matter. They'd been flying at over twenty-thousand feet when the fighter had attacked. Without a chute, Harry wouldn't even feel the impact.

The thin, freezing air roared past his ears as he fell to earth. He glimpsed *Margot* as velocity ripped her to flaming pieces. He said goodbye, to *Margot*, to his parents, to his friends. He couldn't breathe. His vision blurred.

Harry Wakefield slipped into the welcome arms of oblivion.

27 RED

Norman Rolfe considered himself to be a smart man. In fact, he often surprised himself at how smart he really was.

He was smarter than the other punters around the roulette table, frittering away their money while they watched him continue his lucrative winning streak. Six turns of the wheel now, and Rolfe was still winning. He wanted to keep pushing his luck, maybe nine, ten turns, until the towers of coloured chips in front of him soared, but the smart move was to quit while he was ahead. Or in tonight's case, when he got the signal.

Norman had walked into the private gaming club two hours earlier, a vast, smoky basement situated beneath a department store on Chapel Street. He'd bid good evening to the cabbage-eared doormen, flirted with the pretty cloak-room girl as he'd slipped out of his overcoat, smiled at the smartly dressed punters as he'd strolled down the carpeted stairs. His heart had raced, as it always did, when the room opened up before him, a discreetly lit den of vice wrapped in a fog of blue cigarette smoke and crowded with the well-heeled of Liverpool and its environs. The laughter, the drinking, the spin of the wheels, the snap of the cards, the rattle of chips, all of it intoxicated Norman, filling him with an excitement he'd rarely experienced throughout his fifty-seven years. If gambling was a sin, then Norman prayed he'd go straight to hell where the wheels would spin for eternity.

He'd ordered a drink at the bar, a twelve-year-old malt over two cubes and served in a cut-glass tumbler. He'd fired up a Monte Cristo and let the smoky flavours waft around his mouth. He'd smiled at the pretty hostesses as he'd strolled around the tables, then he'd slipped into a recently vacated seat at a blackjack table. He'd changed twenty pounds into chips and started betting small, biding his time, glancing at his watch, at the wide, carpeted staircase. And then, on the stroke of ten, there she was.

Nobody paid Carol Braithwaite any attention. For starters she was an employee, dressed in her croupier uniform of black, knee-length skirt and a stiff-white blouse that was buttoned to the neck. Her blonde hair was tied back into a ponytail, and Norman watched it bob through the crowd until she'd taken over at Roulette Table Number Four. And second, Carol was rather plain, but as far as Norman was concerned that was a minor detail. What *was* important was the love she'd declared for him, the hope she had for their future, and the bitterness she felt for her employer. Tonight would be Carol's last night, and then she would be free, to pursue a life with Norman.

He played a few more hands at the blackjack table, going head-to-head with the dealer, making sure the man remembered him, not as a shrewd card player but as a punter who liked to take risks. Surprisingly, Norman found himself walking away from the table several pounds richer, yet the night was still young. He glanced at his watch as he sauntered through the crowd. Still an hour to kill. He played Baccarat, then a couple of hands of poker, orbiting ever closer to Carol's roulette table like a dying satellite, until he was finally able to squeeze into a chair halfway along its length. Roulette was a popular game at the casino, and Norman could understand why. It took no skill at all, other than a basic knowledge of odds and the belief that luck was either with you or against you. One simply had to pick a number, or a series of numbers, or a colour, and lay a bet. Not exactly brain surgery.

He threw a twenty pound note on the table and waited for his chips. Curious eyes looked in his direction. Carol barely glanced at him.

'Changing twenty,' she announced, sliding the note into the cash slot and pushing his chips towards him. Norman felt a familiar rush of excitement as he arranged the chips in front of him in neat little towers.

And so it went, starting small at first, working up to his first big wager, just as they'd planned. *Five pounds, on black.* Carol spun the wheel. Hungry eyes watched the ball bounce and rattle before settling on a number.

'Fourteen, red.'

Norman heard a few groans around him but he wasn't concerned with that. He was looking at the table, stroking his heavy jowls as he considered his next bet. At least that's what he wanted everyone to think. In fact, he was watching Carol's left hand, waiting for the index digit to tap twice on the polished wood surround—

There.

Two taps, without question. Norman felt his heart race. They were in business.

He bet low again, seemingly stung by the loss of five pounds. Ten shillings on black, five shillings on red, on the corners where the odds were reasonable. The money started to trickle in, a pound here, two pounds there. After forty minutes, Norman was several pounds ahead. Time to shift up a gear.

He placed five pounds on the black diamond and immediately doubled his money. He placed bets on corners and thirds, on colours and rows, odds and evens, winning, losing a little, mixing it up, and the chips soon mounted. A crowd gathered. Punters began shadowing Norman's wagers, and Carol made them pay. No one was hitching a ride on their wagon.

Spin number seven.

The wheel rumbled and the ball rattled, hopping and clacking until it finally settled on...

Twenty-seven red.

Norman had twelve pounds sitting on that very number. A gasp went up around him, and he felt hands slapping his back. Four-hundred and twenty-quid in one turn. Norman hopped excitedly as Carol passed the chips across, adding to the pile in front of him. Spins eight and nine went much the same way, drawing people away from nearby tables. As far as Norman was concerned this was better than sex, not that he'd enjoyed much of that in his life. Tonight though, would be an exception. He'd already booked a hotel room in the city, and when they got there, he'd give Carol a good seeing-to. Well, as much of a seeing-to as a very fat man could give to a trim young thing like Carol. Still, it was all about showing appreciation, and if the sex was below par, a bulging wallet would certainly make up for it.

'One more,' he told the surrounding onlookers, rubbing his hands together. 'One more bet and that's me done for the evening.'

As he said the words, he noticed a couple of tall, thickset men in tuxedos pushing their way through the crowd to the edge of the table. Norman swallowed hard as he stared at his chips. The lunkheads hovered, flaring their flat noses. Another man joined them, a blond, suave-looking type in a much better-fitting tux. He smoked a cigarette as he smiled and stared. Norman looked away, his stomach churning. He glanced at Carol but she had her eyes fixed firmly on her work. Either way, he had to see the bet through.

He placed ten shillings on red. The wheel spun.

'Eleven black,' Carol announced in a voice that barely carried.

There was a disappointed groan. People began drifting away from the table, the spell broken. Mister Suave took his cue.

'Table's closed, ladies and gentlemen. Thank you.'

The crowd drifted away. Suave circled the table without taking his eyes off Norman. He held out his hand. 'Congratulations, Mister...?'

'Rolfe. Norman Rolfe.' Norman kept his head down as he corralled his chips. Carefully constructed towers collapsed beneath trembling fingers.

'You've done well tonight, Mister Rolfe. Let me get you some help.'

Before Norman could protest, Suave was clicking his fingers at one of the lunkheads. 'Ernie, give Mister Rolfe a hand here would you? Let's get him cashed out.' Suave turned to Norman and raised an eyebrow. 'Unless you intend to keep playing? We've only got so much money in the safe you know.' Suave smiled, but his blue eyes were like ice.

Norman faked his own smile. 'No, no, that's fine. Always quit when you're ahead, that's what my father taught me.'

'Wise words,' Suave agreed. He held out his arm. 'Shall we?'

As Norman was escorted away, he glanced over his shoulder. A shiny silk cover had been thrown over the table and Carol had disappeared. At the cashiers desk, the heavies book ended Norman as the cashier counted out his winnings.

'Nine thousand, one hundred and thirty-two pounds, four shillings and sixpence, sir. Congratulations,' she added with a smile.

Norman thanked her, pocketing the thick envelope inside his jacket. *Over nine grand. An absolute fortune.* 'Well, thank you, gentlemen. Good night to you.'

Suave blocked his escape towards the stairs. 'Just a second there, Mister Rolfe. We can't let you go without a small celebration, can we? Why don't you join the other high-rollers in the VIP suite? There's music, complementary food and drink...and girls, of course. D'you like the ladies, Mister Rolfe?'

Norman did. He thought about Carol and realised she must've slipped away while the going was good. She was going to cry off sick, then go straight to the hotel as planned. *Surely a quick drink or two wouldn't hurt?* Besides, it might look suspicious if he scarpered straight off.

'One for the road, then.'

They boxed Norman in and carved their way through

the crowd to a set of double doors. Beyond, a softly lit carpet stretched beneath the building. Norman strode along it, thinking about the girls. Suave pointed to a set of stairs.

'Down there, Mister Rolfe.'

Norman hesitated for just a second, then headed deeper below ground. At the bottom of the staircase his shoes scraped on rough concrete. The walls down here were unpainted, the red brick bare, the corridor long and gloomy. Norman's heart began beating like a rabbit's, and a cold sweat pimpled his forehead. His mind raced. He slowed, patting his jacket.

'I've left my pills in my overcoat,' he said.

A strong hand shoved him in the back. 'Keep moving, chubby.'

Norman bit his lip. *You stupid, stupid man.* Things weren't going to work out, he knew that now. There would be no sailing off into the sunset. He saw an open door, glimpsed crates of beer and wine, and a blood-soaked Carol slumped in a chair—

At the end of the corridor was another room, all naked bulbs, brick walls and puddles on the floor. And a wooden chair. With a rope coiled on the seat. Against the wall was a table, and Norman saw the tools arranged in a neat row; a hammer, pliers, a knuckle duster. The bile rose in his throat and he vomited onto the floor. Suave shoved him hard and Norman fell against the wall, still retching.

'Pick him up.'

Strong hands grabbed his arms and manhandled him into the chair. He heaved vomit into his lap as his hands were tied behind his back. He heard the scrape of a bucket and then freezing cold water hit him in the face. Norman gasped, barely able to catch his breath. He heard footsteps, then the snap of a lighter. Cigarette smoke lingered on the damp, stale air.

'So, how long have you been stealing from me, soft lad?'

Norman closed his eyes. He knew the voice. Everyone knew the voice, a Scouse accent that had been dragged through gravel and dropped into the bottom of a well. Legend told he'd had a faint lisp as a kid, an impediment that people stopped mocking the day fifteen-year-old Jimmy Vaughn beat a man twice his age half to death with a snooker cue. Vaughn had come a long way since then. Nightclubs, casinos, pubs, a caravan park or two, boarding houses down on the coast. And to get it all, Jimmy had lied, cheated, punched, kicked, stabbed, broken limbs, and, if rumours were to be believed, killed people to become one of the most feared gangsters in England. And if those same rumours were true, Jimmy Vaughn hated thieves more than anything. Those that stole from *him*, of course.

Norman heaved again, dry heaves now, his body shaking, his bald dome dotted with sweat. His left arm started to throb, the pain shooting up and down it like an express elevator. A shadow loomed over him. He caught a whiff of cologne and a sharp slap around the face. Suave.

'You heard Mister Vaughn. Answer the question.'

Norman felt weak and his head swam. The pain in his left arm was getting worse and spreading across his chest. 'I need my pills. They're in my coat pocket. In the cloakroom.'

He felt a hand lift his chin, and then Norman was staring up at Jimmy Vaughn. He wasn't a big man, average height, average build, his dark hair cut short, a bite-sized section of flesh missing from his right ear. But there was something about the eyes, Norman realised. Like a scientist looking through a microscope at a specimen. Black eyes too.

He'd once heard someone jokingly refer to Vaughn as the *Angel of Death*. No one had laughed.

Vaughn squeezed his jaw. 'Your little girlfriend says you've been stealing from me for three months. You've been coming here twice a week, so I reckon you've had me for about ten grand. Throw in a bit of interest, you know, for my trouble, and we'll call it a flat twenty. Question is, how you gonna pay, soft lad?'

There was an iron fist inside Norman Rolfe's chest. He felt its cold fingers wrap around his heart and squeeze. His eyes widened as an unspeakable pain shot through his body. The iron fist gripped harder, and Norman imagined blood pouring over the metal fingers. He screamed. Vaughn stepped back. The pain subsided, but Norman knew it wouldn't be for long. He could feel the next wave building, his whole body tingling like he was being pricked with a million needles. His head lolled, and for the briefest of moments, Norman Rolfe remembered a happier time, earlier that evening, when the world had held so much promise. When he thought he was smarter than the rest.

As Norman's heart burst, he realised he wasn't so smart after all.

TREMOR

Harry Wakefield stamped his feet on the mat and closed the farmhouse door behind him, shutting out the cold wind. He shook his coat off and hung it on the rack behind the door. Melting snow dripped on the tiles. He found Beth in the kitchen, stirring something warm and hearty on the stove. Harry kissed her cheek and leaned over her shoulder.

'Smells good. What're we having?'

'Chicken soup.'

'Great. I'm starving.'

He went to the sink and studied his fingernails; they were black with dirt and god-knew-what else. His shoulders ached. In fact, his whole body ached. This was his life now, and Harry Wakefield gave thanks for it every day. It was a far cry from the factory, the coal deliveries, the labouring on building sites, all jobs that Harry hated. He was a hill farmer now, living in a remote yet stunning part of the country. Well, he wasn't *really* a farmer, not yet. They'd only been working the place for three months, but it felt right, and Harry loved the outdoors, the rugged beauty of the surrounding mountains. It was home.

He ran the tap and waited for the water to warm up. Outside the window, the light was fading fast, the land surrendering to shadows and darkness. Fine flakes of snow drifted across the hillside.

'The sheep are a bit skittish this evening.'

'Really? Why?'

Harry shrugged. 'No idea, but that's what Dougie reckons.'

'He should know.' Beth wiped her hands on her apron. 'Charlie's in the sitting room. Go and say hello. Supper's ready in ten minutes.'

It was the cosiest room in the farmhouse, with a thick carpet and comfy chairs arranged before a big stone fireplace. It's where they liked to sit after dinner, talking, listening to the radio, the lights off, the walls flickering with warm firelight. Harry crept to the door and peered around it. Charlie lay in front of the fire, a colouring book spread out in front of him, oblivious to his father's presence. His face was scrunched into a frustrated frown, and Harry felt a familiar rush of emotion. Charlie was an only child, and the fact that Beth couldn't bear any more made him all that more precious.

'Hello, Son.'

Charlie smiled and scrambled to his feet. He threw his arms around Harry's waist. 'Dad.'

Harry squeezed him back. 'What's that you're doing?'

Charlie frowned again. 'Colours.'

Harry picked up the book. It was titled *Animals of Africa,* and was filled with pictures of jungles, forests and watering holes, and the myriad species found there, waiting only for a child and his crayons to bring the pages to life.

Charlie looked up at him with big brown eyes. 'What colour is a lion, Dad?'

Harry's heart ached as he flipped through the book; green zebras, purple grass, houses and tower blocks drawn around an African lagoon. Harry forced a smile. 'Lions are yellow, I suppose. Here.' He offered Charlie a yellow crayon. 'That's yellow.'

The boy took it from him, studied it carefully. Then he smiled. 'I know that, Dad. I'm not stupid.'

Harry winced. *Stupid* was a word little Charlie had heard too many times already throughout his nine short years; at his old school, in the classroom, the playground, in the pub back in Ilkeston, where Harry had overheard one of the locals making fun of his son. Harry had broken the man's nose.

He watched Charlie lay back down and colour the lion with the yellow crayon. Halfway through he stopped to admire his work. 'It doesn't look right,' he said, then he picked up a black crayon and coloured the rest of the animal in.

Harry bit his lip. The doctor's were baffled too. *He'll grow out of it,* that was the considered medical opinion, and Harry prayed they were right. He held out his hand. 'C'mon, Son, leave that for now. Let's wash up for dinner.'

Charlie obeyed without question. He got to his feet and held his dad's hand. 'Will you tell me a story at bedtime?'

'We'll see.'

They ate supper in the kitchen, and Charlie told his Mum and Dad about his day at the village school. He'd settled in okay, but there'd been a few problems. Charlie needed more attention than the other kids, which troubled them both. Despite the move from a big town in Derbyshire to a small Welsh village clinging to the foothills of the Berwyn Mountains, Charlie's problems continued to dog him. The kids still poked fun, and the teachers found him a little difficult to tcach because he didn't always pick things up straight away. Life was going to be tough for little Charlie, but they'd get through it, as a family. Eventually.

After the dishes were cleared and Charlie had gone upstairs, Beth took a seat at the table. Harry poured them both a small whiskey.

'There's a play on the radio at nine,' she told him. 'Thought we might have a listen.'

Harry sipped his drink. 'Sure, but I'm going to pop back out first, check on the animals.'

'Okay. Don't be too long.' They enjoyed a comfortable silence for a minute or two, then Beth said, 'It could be a real struggle this winter. We'll have to work hard. Harder than we ever have.'

'We knew this wouldn't be easy,' he agreed. 'Just a pity Norman didn't keel over in the spring.' He grinned, holding up his hands. 'I'm joking, love. But we've been lucky though, right?'

'Yes,' Beth agreed, 'and thank god we've got Dougie and the boys to run the place.'

'We'd be lost without them.'

Beth got to her feet and took Harry's empty glass. 'If you're going out, go. Make sure you're back for the play. I'll put Charlie to bed.'

After wrapping up in his winter gear, Harry stepped outside and headed for the track that ran past the house. Beth was right, they'd have to work hard this winter. As a business the farm kept its head above water, but Beth's uncle Norman had become a little careless in the months before his death. The books were a mess and the bank account had taken a mild beating, but the farm was still solvent and there would be opportunities to improve their fortunes in the spring. All in all, Lady Luck had smiled on them.

Night had fallen, and low clouds moved like grey spectres across the hills. Grass and stone walls glistened as sleet swept through Harry's torch beam. To his right, the track headed down towards Dougie's cottage, and the equipment sheds and barns. A mile beyond that, lost in the darkness of the valley below, stood the village of Finnhagel. To Harry's left, the track headed uphill, dissecting the farm's topmost fields before plunging into a thick pine forest that guarded the summit at Craggan Peak, a barren, windswept mountain that looked west towards the foothills of Snowdonia.

Harry crossed the track to the stone wall and swept his torch out across the field. Frightened eyes stared back at him. The sheep moved around in a nervous herd, stopping and starting, bleating fitfully. Harry was no expert, but even he could see they were scared.

He'd heard rumours of wolves and bears in these mountains, but that's all they were, rumours, and Beth had poured scorn on the notion. She'd spent whole summers on the farm as a kid, but for a townie like Harry, living in a remote farmhouse took some getting used to. He loved the days, which kept him busy from dawn until dusk, but the nights were silent, the fields dark and often foreboding. A couple of hundred yards up the track the ancient forest added its own menace, and sometimes Harry imagined cold eyes watching the house from its black shadows. Beth said he had an overactive imagination. Harry agreed, but that didn't make him feel any easier.

So he trudged up towards the forest, because the more

he realised his fear was irrational, the quicker he'd get used to country life. He swept his torch across the fields on either side, catching glimpses of huddled sheep herds. A rumble rolled across the hills, and Harry stopped and turned around. The house was barely visible in the distance, marked only by the unnatural angle of its roof. The rumble faded to nothing. *Odd,* he thought, as he continued up the track.

The forest loomed ahead, its massed ranks of thick pines guarding the entrance to the peak. The wind picked up, moaning through the trees. Branches creaked and groaned. Ahead, the track disappeared into complete darkness.

Something moved out of the corner of his eye—

Harry spun around, torch waving. He heard twigs snapping and his torch beam picked out the spindly legs of a deer as it scampered between the trees and disappeared into the shadows. He smiled to himself, his heart beating fast inside his chest. *Time to go, Harry.*

Back in the house he bolted the front door and hung up his coat. He poured another couple of whiskies and sat down with Beth in the sitting room. They tuned in the radio and listened to the play on the BBC. They laughed a lot, and afterwards they spent a while chatting before drifting into a comfortable silence. They watched the flames die in the hearth. They were in bed by ten-thirty, asleep by ten-forty.

Dead to the world.

'HARRY! WAKE UP!'

His eyes snapped open. The bed was shaking. No, Harry realised; the whole room was shaking. He threw back the blankets and swung his feet to the cold wooden floor. Not just the room—

The whole house was shuddering. He heard a couple of tiles slide down the roof and shatter on the cobbles below. Pictures on the walls rattled. Everything seemed to be moving. He threw open the door and Charlie was standing outside, bare feet, pyjamas, eyes wide. 'Dad, what's happening?'

Harry pulled him into the bedroom. Beth was already half-dressed in trousers and a thick jumper. 'Beth, take Charlie outside, away from the house.'

She scooped the boy up and took him downstairs. Harry pulled on his clothes. Beth's night creams and perfumes marched across the sideboard and toppled to the floor.

And then it stopped.

Harry stood motionless, listening, then he went to the window and yanked the curtains back. There was no giant chasm in the road outside, no wall of mud coming down the mountain towards them. There was nothing but silence.

Then something caught Harry's eye. The sky above Craggan Peak throbbed with a faint green glow—

The moor was on fire.

He buttoned up his shirt and ran downstairs. Beth was in the hallway, pulling on a coat. Charlie stood next to her, bundled up in a duffel coat, hat and boots.

'Careful,' she pointed. 'Glass on the floor. The pictures came off the wall.'

Harry stepped around and slipped on his boots. 'There's a fire up on the peak,' he told her. 'I think it's a plane crash.'

Beth's eyes widened. 'A what?'

'I'll drive up there, make sure it's on our side of the mountain. You take Charlie down to Dougie's and call the police from there. Tell them what happened but don't mention a plane crash, not until I've seen it with my own eyes. The last thing we need is to send people in the wrong direction.'

'Don't do anything stupid,' she warned. 'Come on Charlie. Let's go and see Aunt Rita.'

There were two beaten-up Land Rovers parked outside the farmhouse. Harry climbed in one and fired up the engine, crunching it into gear. Beth and Charlie got into the other and drove off down the hill, disappearing into the darkness.

Harry switched on the lights and drove towards the forest. The Rover bounced its way along the track, densely packed trees towering on either side. The gravel was wet and slippery, and a couple of times the back-end fishtailed around slippery bends. Harry slowed down, forcing himself to think about what he might face when he got up there.

Whatever it was, it had shaken the whole mountain. That meant it was probably one of those big jet airliners, like a VC 10. A high-speed crash with multiple fatalities. There would be mangled bodies and luggage everywhere, not to mention twisted metal and burning jet fuel. And Harry would be first on the scene.

He wiped the condensation away from the windshield. He could see the sky through the trees now, still glowing an intense, lurid green, which struck Harry as odd. The pines began to thin out as they marched towards the summit, and he gripped the wheel a little tighter as the Rover climbed the last couple of hundred feet towards the edge of the moor. He slowed down, conscious of potential survivors who might stagger into his path.

Easy, Harry.

The trees finally surrendered to a vast, undulating landscape of snow-covered ferns that reached up to the jagged peak. The Rover skidded to a halt and Harry threw the door open, stumbling out across the moor. The sky over the peak throbbed like the Northern Lights.

And then he saw it, the aircraft, its nose part-buried in the hillside, leaving a wide, muddy scar a couple of hundred yards long in its wake. The plane was huge, black against the snow, its tail end glowing green and pointing towards the sky. Harry ran through the ferns towards it. As his eyes became accustomed to the dark, he slowed. And stopped.

Not an aeroplane.

Something else entirely.

CASUALTY

When Beth arrived at Dougie Booth's cottage, the farm manager was already outside in the cobbled courtyard with the farmhands, Ewan and Colin. All of them were looking up at the peak. Dougie's wife Rita, a coat wrapped over her dressing gown, stood at the door.

'Did you feel it?' Beth asked them.

Dougie nodded. 'Earthquake, I reckon. I felt one before, in the Far East, just after the war. Exactly the same.'

'Harry thought it might be a plane crash. He's gone up there to have a look.' As Beth said it, she noticed that the sky over the peak wasn't as green as it had been. In fact, she could barely see any light at all.

'I've called the police,' Dougie told her. 'They knew about the earthquake already. Seems a lot of people have called in. They said they'd send someone up from Oswestry as soon as they could.'

'There might be people up there,' Beth fretted. 'Women, children, all terribly injured.'

'Harry's right, best wait until we know what's what before we call the cavalry.'

Rita took Charlie's hand. 'Come on, little fella, let's get you some lemonade and a biscuit.'

Dougie pulled a bunch of keys from his pocket. 'I'll take a run up there, just in case Harry needs help.'

'I'm coming with you,' Beth told him. 'I was a first-aider, back at the factory in Ilkeston.'

Dougie stopped her with a raised hand. 'I appreciate that, Miss Beth, but Charlie needs you close and Rita's a bit nervy. If we find any walking wounded, we'll bring 'em back. Rita knows where everything is.'

Dougie climbed into his Land Rover and the farmhands piled in the back. The engine rattled into life, wipers squeaking across the windshield, and Beth watched it turn out of the courtyard and head up the hill. She waited until its lights had disappeared from view, and then she waited a moment longer, listening, watching the sky. The green glow had faded to nothing. Silence blanketed the mountain once again.

As if nothing had happened at all.

HARRY'S BREATH froze on the cold air while his legs refused to take him any closer. He smacked his torch several times but it wouldn't work. The black craft towered above him. It wasn't a plane, of that he was certain, because he'd seen this type of craft before, only much, much bigger. The night they were shot down.

The night of the fall.

This craft was smaller, maybe fifty feet long, the nose crumpled and covered in snow and mud. And like the object he'd seen all those years ago, there were no windows, no wings, no tail or visible cockpit. A black airship, like no other. Harry thought back to that night in the Lancaster, when the other craft had swept out of the clouds and appeared alongside them, how it had ducked beneath their bomber and sped away, as if it were playing with them. Harry remembered feeling astonishment, a sense of almost childlike wonder, but not fear. Who or whatever was flying the craft that night was not a threat.

But this was different. He was completely alone, and the sheer strangeness of the craft intimidated him. He felt a slight trembling in the ground beneath his feet, and he heard a hissing sound coming from the recess at the back of the craft. And it no longer glowed.

He circled the crumpled metal of what he assumed was the nose. He moved closer, the craft looming above him, blotting out the stars. Slowly, he reached out and laid a hand on its surface. It was neither cold nor warm, just incredibly smooth to the touch. Like touching glass.

Hissss—

Harry scrambled away through the ferns. There was a blast of air, then a swishing sound, like someone moving through the undergrowth on the other side of the craft. Harry moved up the hill and around the buried nose—

And saw a small figure looking directly at him, arms held out as if trying to steady itself. The shadow swayed for a moment, then collapsed into the snow.

A child, in desperate trouble.

Harry ran to the child's side. It was lying face down, hands grasping at the ferns. Harry saw the figure was bald, its skull extended at the back. Not a child, then.

'It's okay, help is here.'

Harry knelt down, the snow soaking his trousers. The figure wore a dark, one-piece suit, smooth and shiny, and Harry placed gentle hands on the casualty's shoulder and leg, easing him onto his back. Man or boy, he was incredibly skinny. His head lolled over and he looked directly at Harry—

Harry scrambled away, hands and boots clawing the earth as he got to his feet and ran, crashing headlong through the ferns, desperate to escape. His legs pounded and his arms pumped like pistons, bolting across open ground towards the distant Land Rover. He stumbled once, falling headlong, but that didn't stop Harry. He rolled to his feet and kept going, oblivious to the snow, the darkness, his only thought, escape.

His boots slid across the gravel and he yanked the Rover's door open. He slammed it behind him, heart pounding, his wide eyes searching the darkness outside, his fingers fumbling with the ignition key. He turned it and gunned the engine. As his hand wrestled with the gear lever, a voice behind him said, *'Help me.'*

Harry cried out and threw open the door. He fell to the gravel and was back on his feet in an instant, backing away from the vehicle. He watched it idle on the track, door open, headlamps pointing up towards the summit of the peak. Harry struggled to control his fear. He took small, careful steps back towards the Rover. He peered inside. Empty.

'Please...'

Harry spun around. In the distance, the black craft stuck out of the ground like an ancient obelisk.

'Help me...'

And then Harry knew. The casualty, whatever it was, was talking to him inside his head, like a voice on the telephone. He'd never been so frightened in his life. Not even when he was falling through the sky.

He knew what he was facing, and the realisation almost overwhelmed him. He'd read a few books on the subject, and several newspaper articles. He'd even been to the cinema with Beth and watched a couple of Hollywood films. But this was the real thing, just like that night over Germany.

He just looks different, that's all. Don't be scared.

Harry took a deep breath and struck out across the moor.

THINNER

HE WAS BACK behind the wheel of the Land Rover, barrelling down the track.

The pilot—for some reason Harry referred to him as such—was wrapped in a blanket and strapped into the seat next to him. Harry had no idea what was wrong with him and the pilot hadn't spoken a word since he'd muttered *thank you* inside Harry's skull.

The forest flashed by on either side, a tunnel of dark, towering pines squeezing the track ahead. The Rover's tyres bit into the gravel as Harry pumped the brakes for another bend. As he rounded the curve he saw headlights driving up towards him. He hit the brakes and crunched to a stop. The approaching jeep pulled up short. The driver's door opened and a dark figure stepped in front of the lights.

'You okay, Harry?'

Harry closed the gap between them. 'Pull your jeep over, Dougie. And don't go up there, not until the police get here.'

Dougie stepped closer. 'What is it, then? A plane crash?'

Harry shook his head. 'Something else. Military,' he lied. 'Where's Beth?'

Dougie jerked a thumb over his shoulder. 'She's with Rita. They're getting things ready, just in case.'

'Go and tell her I need her back at the house. Right away, Dougie.'

The farm manager stood his ground. 'What's going on?'

'Just do as I ask, okay?'

Dougie shielded his eyes as he squinted into Harry's headlights. 'Who's that you've got with you?'

'No one,' Harry blustered. 'It's just some old sacks. Move your jeep. Quickly!'

Dougie grumbled something and climbed back behind the wheel. He pulled hard across the track, allowing Harry to squeeze the Rover past, and then he was clear, hurtling down the mountain as fast as he could.

The Rover left the darkness of the forest and the valley opened up before him. Harry slowed for the turn through the farmhouse gate and brought the vehicle to a hard stop. He opened the passenger door and gently picked up the pilot, still wrapped in the blanket. Harry couldn't look at him, not this close. The sheer strangeness of the being in his arms frightened him. He backed through the front door and into the hallway. He stamped upstairs, barely exerting himself, the pilot weighing only about the same as Charlie. He kicked open the door to the spare bedroom and gently laid the casualty on the bare mattress. He wrapped an eiderdown around him then dragged the curtains closed and snapped on the bedside light. He ran back downstairs and grabbed a basket of firewood. Within five minutes he had a decent fire building in the grate, and already he could feel the room warming.

Now what?

He steeled himself and approached the bed. He (*she?*) was swaddled in the eiderdown like a baby. Only its face was visible, the strangest face that Harry had ever laid eyes on. It was pale and hairless, with eyes that were large and swept upwards, like an Oriental, although there were no whites to them, just black orbs. There was no nose, instead two nostril-like openings, and the mouth was thin and lip-less. Suddenly those strange eyes blinked, and Harry took an involuntary step back.

'What can I do?' he blurted. 'Where are you hurt?'

'*Water,*' said the voice inside his head.

Harry bolted from the room and charged back down to the kitchen. As he filled a glass, he heard a vehicle outside. Through the window he caught a glimpse of Dougie's jeep racing past the house.

Back upstairs he propped the pilot up on some pillows and helped him sip the water slowly. Neither of them spoke, and Harry was grateful for that. Voices in the head took some getting used to.

The pilot's eyes fluttered nervously as the front door slammed downstairs.

'It's okay. It's my wife and son,' Harry told him, not knowing if that meant anything at all. He forced a smile, hoping that might help. 'I'll be back.'

Harry closed the bedroom door and intercepted them down in the hallway. He held a finger to his lips. 'Let's keep the noise down, okay?'

Beth frowned. 'What's going on? Dougie and the boys look like they've seen a ghost.'

Harry knelt down, took off Charlie's coat and hat. 'You run on up to bed, Son. You can brush your teeth in the morning.' He watched Charlie scamper upstairs and waited until he heard his bedroom door close. Then he turned to Beth. *Where do I start?*

'What is it? What's going on?'

Harry reached out and squeezed Beth's hands. 'You're going to have to steel yourself, love.'

She snatched her hands back. 'You're scaring me.'

'It wasn't a plane that crashed up on the peak. It was something else. A machine. Not from here.'

'What d'you mean? It's foreign?'

'About as foreign as it gets.' He pointed to the ceiling. 'From up there.'

Beth stared at Harry for several moments, her eyes boring into his, her brow knotted with disbelief. 'What are you saying? That it's not...that it's—'

'Alien,' he whispered.

Beth opened her mouth to say something, then stopped herself. She shook her head. 'It's dark up there, Harry. You're mistaken.'

'I touched it. It's real. Just like the one I saw during the war, only smaller.' He took a step closer and grabbed her arms. 'Beth, listen to me. One of the crew, he's injured. I brought him back here. He's upstairs in the spare room.'

Beth stared at him for several, long moments. 'What?'

'I don't even know if it's a him or not. I brought him back because he needs help.'

Beth raised her eyes to the ceiling. 'There's someone upstairs? In the spare bedroom?'

Harry nodded. 'You'd better brace yourself. It takes some getting used to. Oh, and when he talks you can hear it in your head. Like a voice on the telephone.'

'What?'

Harry shook her. Not hard, but enough to get her attention. 'Beth, I need you to focus, okay? It doesn't matter what

35

he looks like or where he's from. He needs your help. Please.'

Harry let go. Beth took several deep breaths. Finally she said, 'Okay,' and disappeared into the kitchen. When she returned, she was carrying the first-aid box. 'Show me.'

Harry led the way. The spare room had warmed considerably, and the pilot turned his head towards them. Harry stood to one side and watched his wife's face as she laid eyes on their houseguest. She paled, her face almost matching the pilot's skin tone. She put a hand to her mouth, her feet rooted to the floorboards. Harry knew exactly what she was feeling.

'Don't be afraid. You are not in any danger.'

Beth gasped behind her hand.

'See?' Harry said. He watched his wife take a deep breath and walk towards the edge of the bed. When she spoke, her voice shook.

'My name is Beth. I'm going to examine you, is that okay?'

'I have contusions to my lower limbs. The injuries are slight, but my body requires water and organic materials to accelerate the healing process.'

Harry saw his wife's hands shaking, but the pilot was using words that were familiar; *contusions, injuries, healing.* Words that could anchor her, focus her mind. Beth was strong, he knew that. She'd push on through.

The pilot's eyes blinked. Beth removed the eiderdown and now Harry saw the pilot properly for the first time. He guessed his height at around five feet tall, with a head that looked slightly larger and out of proportion with his body. He was dressed in a silvery-grey, one-piece overall that was tight fitting with a high, round collar, and he wore thin boots on his feet. Harry noticed his fingers, three of them on each hand, the digits elongated. Human-ish, but so very different.

'Harry, go check on Charlie.' Beth was staring at him, nodding towards the door.

Harry took the hint and left the room. He crept along the landing and looked in on Charlie, who was already sound asleep. The evening's excitement had clearly taken its toll on the boy, and Harry debated whether to keep him out-of-school tomorrow. Just one of many decisions he would have to make before the sun rose.

Down in the kitchen he filled the kettle and heated it up on the stove. By the time its whistle filled the kitchen, Beth had reappeared. She rummaged in the larder without a word, then went back upstairs carrying a jug of water and a cabbage. Harry made another cup of tea and waited. Beth returned twenty minutes later. She closed the kitchen door behind her and dropped into a chair at the table. She stared at the wood, her head shaking. Finally she looked at Harry.

'I can't believe it,' she whispered. 'He's not human. He's like us, but he's not. It's hard to explain. It's hard to understand—'

'Here, get that down you.' Harry handed her a mug of sweet tea. Beth unscrewed the whiskey bottle and added a splash to both their drinks.

'Oh my God,' she whispered between sips, still struggling with what she'd seen.

'How is he? Is he badly injured?'

Beth shook her head. 'I don't think so. He told me what to do, how to treat his wounds. He doesn't have blood, not like us. His legs are like plant stalks, you know, rubbery, only pale and thin. He explained that his muscles were more like the fibres of a plant, that they would knit together somehow. I've wrapped his wounds in cabbage leaves, for God's sake.' She shook her head again, dumbfounded.

'We have to think about what we do next,' Harry warned.

'What d'you mean?'

Harry took a sip of his tea. 'I didn't tell Dougie about our guest. I don't know why. I just have a feeling that if people found out, they'd treat him like some kind of Frankenstein's monster. What did you tell the police?'

'Dougie had already phoned them. They knew about the earthquake already.'

'Did he mention a crash of any sorts?' Beth shook her head. 'Okay, that'll buy us a little time to think. They need to be told, though. There's a bloody great flying machine lying up there and we can't have people scrambling all over it. Could be dangerous. Radiation, that sort of thing.'

'You touched it,' Beth realised.

'I know. I think I'm okay, though.'

'So, what do we do?'

'We speak to the pilot—'

'He's the *pilot*?'

'I don't know. Maybe. It's his aircraft. If there's any danger—'

Bang! Bang! Bang!

The thumping shook the whole house. Out in the hall-way, Harry and Beth saw a shadow moving beyond the opaque glass of the front door. When Harry opened it, Dougie pushed past him into the hallway. He pulled the cap off his head and rounded on them, his voice rising.

'You saw it! Didn't you, Harry? I know you did! Jesus Christ, what the bloody hell is that thing?'

Beth put a finger to her lips. 'Be quiet, Dougie, for God's sake. You'll wake Charlie up.'

The farm manager was like a cat on a hot tin roof. He couldn't stand still, his head shaking, the words tumbling from his mouth. 'Damnedest thing I ever saw. A flying saucer, that's what it was. From outer space. Maybe they're Martians.'

Harry frowned. '*They?*'

Dougie nodded several times. 'Young Colin got inside, had a look around. He said he saw bodies, little ones, like kids. Said they were all dead.'

Harry's jaw dropped. 'He went *inside?*'

'He didn't last long. Came scrambling out like he had a firework us his arse. Terrified, he was. He still ain't right.'

'I told you not to go up there,' Harry told him.

Dougie scowled. 'You might be the boss around here, but the peak's common ground. If I want to look, I'll damn well do as I please. Glad I did too. That sort of thing you only see once in your lifetime.' The farm manager shook his head. 'My God, to think all that science fiction nonsense is true. Hard to get your head around.' He slapped his cap back on and opened the front door. 'I called the station at Oswestry again, told them what was up there. That put the wind up 'em.'

'Let's keep this to ourselves for now,' Harry warned. 'We don't want the people panicking, do we?'

'Fat chance of that,' Dougie scoffed. 'Colin and Ewan took off down to the village like a pair of bloody greyhounds. They'll have heard about this in Wrexham by the time the sun comes up.'

'I'm not so sure.'

Both men looked down the hallway, to where Beth was standing by the phone. She was holding the receiver in her hand.

'The phone's dead.'

MINISTRY OF AIR

His name was Peter Nash, and he was a Group Captain in the Royal Air Force, although he hadn't worn a uniform for several years.

He worked out of a small office on the third-floor of the Air Ministry building in London, an office that bore no signage, no nameplate or number. Just a door with a panel of frosted glass, a door that was thick and heavy and always locked from the inside.

Nash ran a team of two men and one woman. Sergeant Gladys Smith was an RAF veteran of twelve years and the best transcriber Nash had ever worked with. She sat behind her desk, headphones clamped over her ears as she typed up a tape recording of a BOAC pilot who'd encountered an unidentified flying machine at thirty-two thousand feet over Greenland. The machine had been silent, with no visible markings, and according to both the pilot and his navigator, had been roughly the size of a cruise ship. The pilots were reminded of the need for secrecy, underpinned by the very real threat of having their licences revoked. Nash was certain that, like so many others, these two men would come to their senses and keep their mouths firmly shut.

Gladys' face was impassive, her fingers hammering the typewriter keys with impressive speed. She saw Nash watching her and winked. Nash smiled. What Gladys lacked in looks she made up for with a sense of humour and stoic professionalism. She was also a first-class logistics coordinator, and in the armed forces, people like that were worth their weight in gold.

Nash went back to the *Recent Sightings* file he was reading. Most of them were reports submitted by the public and could be explained away by a variety of ground, weather and atmospheric phenomena. But sightings were on the rise, and Nash and his team had to provide explanations creative enough to satisfy society's growing curiosity.

He looked up as he heard a faint tapping from out in the corridor, growing louder and more urgent with each second. He stared at the door, waiting. A moment later it flew open and Corporal Syd Phelan skidded into the room in polished brogues. He closed the door behind him and stood in front of Nash's desk, breathless. In his hand was a message slip.

'Just took a call at the main switchboard, Mister Nash. From the Duty Sergeant at Oswestry police station. They've received several reports from just over the Welsh border, a village called Finnhagel, in the Berwyn Mountains. Initial reports were of an earthquake, but now a local farmer has reported a crash on the peak above the village. Called it a *spaceship*. Said there were bodies too.' Phelan handed over the message.

Nash scanned it, got to his feet, his heart beating fast. *This could be it. What they'd all been waiting for.*

'You know the drill, Syd. Let's start with the local tele-

41

phone exchange, get it shut down. And every exchange it links to.'

'Already done, Mister Nash. Also told the Duty Sergeant to wake up his people and seal off all approaches to the alleged crash site. Apparently it's pretty remote, so containment should be easy enough.'

'Good lad.'

'What's going on?'

It was Gladys, holding one of her headphones away from her ear.

'Suspected *Fallen Angel*. Call Ron, would you Gladys? And we'll need immediate transportation.'

Nash gave her the message slip and Gladys speed-read it as she dialled a number with her pencil. Nash and Phelan went to their respective lockers at the other end of the room and grabbed their overnight bags. Pulling on their hats and overcoats at the door, Nash looked expectantly at Gladys as she wound up another phone call.

'There's a car waiting outside to take you to Biggin Hill. A C-47 will fly you north to Rednal Aerodrome. It's an old RAF training facility, about twenty miles from the village. Bill's on his way. He's mobilised the recovery team and will meet you at the airfield.'

Nash nodded. 'I want our people all over that mountain before anyone else sees what's up there.'

'What about Condor?'

'Don't call them yet. Not until we've confirmed either way.'

They left Gladys to do what she did best; organise people and logistics. Nash and his team would be first on scene. Well, the first government people at least.

The car was waiting out on Whitehall. Traffic was light, and with their police escort racing ahead, they made it to the airfield in under an hour. The C-47 Skytrain was waiting for them on the apron, propellers running. Ron Chambers, Nash's security officer, waited for them at the bottom of the steps. They shook hands quickly before boarding the aircraft.

Then they were on the move, thundering down the runway and lifting off into the clear night sky.

FIRM HANDED

THE VILLAGE of Finnhagel clung to the lower slopes of the mountain and was home to just over a hundred and fifty people, most of them living in grey stone houses clustered around a small high street that boasted several shops, a small church and a single pub. *The Griffin* had won the battle for the soul of the village a long time ago, a warm and welcoming gathering place for Finnhagel's close-knit community.

Around the back of the pub was a small car park, and the sleek black Mercedes Benz 600 saloon turned into the courtyard and parked nose-first against a stone wall. The headlamps blinked out and all four doors opened. Luggage was retrieved from the boot, and four well-dressed men headed for the back entrance of the pub. The man in front, a suave-looking blond gentleman in a dark overcoat, opened the door and allowed the smaller man behind him to pass inside.

Jimmy Vaughn strolled into the bar and looked around. *Cosy*, was his first impression. Nice big fire, stone floors, chairs with cushions, a dartboard room, and a well-lit bar area with a decent selection of optics. His second impression was, *ignorant carrot-crunchers*. Five of them in fact, two polishing glasses behind the bar and three toothless old duffers on stools, all staring at Vaughn and his friends.

'We're closed I'm afraid,' said the man behind the bar, a balding, ruddy-faced yokel with ginger mutton-chops and a belly hanging over his belt.

Vaughn leaned on the bar and smiled. 'You must be the guvnor?'

'That's right. Gavin Souter's the name. This is my wife, Meg.'

Vaughn ignored the introduction. 'We need rooms, three of them, for a couple of nights. One each for me and my colleague here. The other lads will share.'

'A couple of nights, you say?' Souter reached beneath the counter and placed a thick diary on the bar. He licked his thumb and flicked the pages over. 'Let's have a look, shall we?'

Souter's wife was staring at Terry O'Gorman. She was a large lady, all hips and tits, the latter straining at her white shirt, her skin leathery and caked in make-up. *Mutton dressed as lamb,* Vaughn decided. A lot of women did that. Stared at Terry. He was a good-looking lad, like a film star, some said. Terry always got the girls. He liked to hurt them too. Vaughn had watched him slice the face off several over the years. Very skilled with a cutthroat razor, was our Terry.

Vaughn glanced at the landlord, at the empty pages of his diary. He reached into his overcoat and pulled out his wallet. He flapped it open, and that got Souter's attention because it was stuffed with notes. Vaughn extracted one of them and slapped it on the bar.

'We've had a long drive, so lets cut the nonsense and get those rooms, eh, lad?'

Souter nodded, transfixed by the twenty-pound note pinned to the bar with Vaughn's finger. He pushed it towards the landlord. 'We'll need something to eat too. Take care of us and you'll be well looked after. That suit you?'

Vaughn took his finger off the note and Souter pocketed it with impressive speed. 'Not a problem, Mister...?'

'Vaughn.'

Souter's wife beamed a mouthful of yellowed crockery at him. 'You're all big lads,' she smiled, her eyes fixed on Terry. 'Rugby team, is it?'

'Scousers,' one of the old duffers at the bar chipped in. 'Don't get many of your lot round 'ere, not during winter.'

Vaughn was about to reply when the pub door flew open and two young men bundled inside. Vaughn's hand slipped inside his coat, his fingers gripping the handle of the short cosh nestled in its specially made pocket. Terry had moved to Vaughn's side, ready for trouble, but after a quick appraisal, Vaughn relaxed. They were youngsters, kids really. And they were already scared.

'Did you feel it?' one of the boys blabbed. He was the bigger of the two, with jug ears and a mop of black hair. 'Tell us you felt it, Gavin.'

Souter gave his wife a sideways glance. 'You mean that earthquake? Of course we bloody felt it. Meg dropped a handful of glasses.'

'Gave me a proper fright,' she said, giggling nervously and glancing at Terry.

'It wasn't an earthquake.'

The bar went quiet as Jug Ears planted his hands on the bar, his chest heaving. The smaller, skinny kid looked like he was shaking. Souter poured them both a finger of scotch and they emptied their glasses in one tip.

'Tell us what it was, then.'

'Something crashed, up on the peak. A spaceship.'

There was a moment of absolute silence. The old duffers nudged each other, smirks on their faces. 'You boys been drinking?' one of them chuckled.

Jug Ears turned on them. 'We seen it with our own eyes! Great big bloody thing it was. No wings, no windows, nothing.'

'Might be one of those satellites,' Vaughn offered. The boys stared. So did the old duffers. Even Terry was giving Vaughn a curious glance.

Jug Ears shook his head. 'No, mate. It's a spaceship, and its got people in it too. Martians, probably.'

That got the codgers laughing again. Even Souter was grinning. Vaughn wiped the smiles from all their faces.

'I'll give you twenty quid each if you take me up there.'

Curious eyes flicked from Vaughn to the boys and back again. It wasn't Jug Ears who answered this time, it was the other one, the skinny kid.

'You don't want to see that, mister.'

'Colin crawled inside it,' Jug Ears told them all, slapping a hand on his friend's shoulder. 'He saw those things. They're all dead, right Colin?'

The skinny kid nodded. Vaughn knew fear when he saw it, and he'd seen plenty. He knew when people were lying too. These boys were on the level. Whatever they'd seen, Vaughn wanted in.

'Fifty quid each.'

Toothless jaws dropped open.

'I'll take you,' Souter announced. 'Meg, go get my car keys.'

'We ain't said *no* yet,' Jug Ears protested.

A pale blue light swept the walls of the pub. Colin cringed, cowering behind Jug Ears. The roar filled the room, the wailing sirens, and then the police cars were sweeping past the windows.

'Bloody hell,' scowled Souter.

'They're heading up to the peak,' Jug Ears said. 'You won't get anywhere near it now.'

Souter cursed. Vaughn peeled a five pound note from his wallet and laid it on the bar. 'Give these boys whatever they want,' he told the landlord. 'The old fellers too. And have one yourself.'

Souter brightened. 'Right you are, Mister Vaughn. Meg, show our guests to their rooms and get them fed.'

Vaughn took Terry to one side. 'Get Vic and Pat to take the cases upstairs. You and me will hang about down here, friend up the locals.'

'Were you serious?' Terry asked in a low voice. 'About paying them kids?'

'Course I was. Why?'

Terry grinned. 'Spaceships, Jimmy? You're not going soft in the head, are ya?'

Vaughn glared at his consigliere. 'I've read books, see? Written by professors and that. Clever blokes. Educated. If they think these things are real, that's good enough for me.'

'Fair enough,' Terry caved.

Vaughn nodded across the bar, his voice low. 'Let's assume these two twats are telling the truth, which I'm betting they are. How much d'you think something like that is worth, eh? I'll tell ya. Millions. And what about the bodies? Imagine taking one of 'em around the world, charging people to come see it. We'd be richer than the Royal Family, mate. It's what they call a business opportunity.'

'What about the other thing? The debt?'

'That's still a priority, but this spaceship lark could

prove to be a very lucrative bonus, so we'll keep our eyes and ears open. Get the drinks, lad.'

Vaughn walked around the bar and offered his hand to Jug Ears and Colin. 'A pleasure to meet you boys. My name's Jimmy. Let's take a pew by the fire, get you warmed up. Then you can tell me all about this spaceship, eh?'

SKYTRAIN

THE DOOR SLAMMED, shaking the house again. Harry and Beth stood in the hall, speechless in the wake of Dougie's angry departure. It was Beth who spoke first.

'I've never seen Dougie act that way before.'

'He's scared,' Harry told her. 'I am too, to be honest.'

'Not as scared as our houseguest, I'll bet. I'll look in on him. You get this glass swept up.'

Harry grabbed a dustpan and brush from the cupboard and swept the hall. Satisfied that a shoeless Charlie wouldn't cut himself on any stray slivers, Harry bolted the front door and turned the lights off downstairs. He found Beth standing at the end of the pilot's bed.

'It's late,' he whispered. 'We should keep our voices down. The last thing we need is Charlie walking in here unannounced.'

Harry wasn't sure if any of that made sense to the creature in the bed. *Creature* seemed a harsh word to use because this was a highly intelligent being he was referring to, but Harry wasn't sure what other word to use. Time to find out.

'What do we call you?' Harry tapped his chest with a finger. 'My name is Harry, Harry Wakefield. This is my wife Beth. We have a son, Charlie. We're a family. What shall we call you?'

'Vela.'

Beth looked at Harry, then the pilot. 'Vela?'

The pilot's eyes blinked, and his voice echoed in their heads. *'My full name is not translatable in any of your Earth languages.'*

'Vela it is, then.' Harry bit his lip and said, 'There were others with you, in your ship. Is there anything we can do?'

Vela shook his head. *'Their bodies have expired, but long ago we learnt to capture and store the electrical impulses that you call memory and consciousness. These can be viewed, or transferred to other hosts.'* Vela pulled a thin arm from beneath the eiderdown and held up a small square of glass, the size of a playing card. Harry looked closer. Inside the glass, tiny worms of light glittered inside.

'What the hell is that?'

'My crew. Their impulses. I must return them.'

Beth gripped the metal bed frame. 'Where are you from? Why are you here, on Earth?'

'And your ship, how is it powered?,' Harry wanted to know.

Vela tucked the glass card away. *'My energy levels are low and require replenishment. We can continue after your Earth cycles.'*

'You mean, in the morning?' Beth asked him.

'The morning, yes.'

Vela blinked his eyes and Beth shooed Harry from the room. 'We'll leave you to rest,' she told him.

As Harry opened the door, he heard Vela's voice in his head.

'Your leaders will send people to find me. I will not be safe, not until I can get to a portal.'

'What the hell's a *portal*?' Harry asked. 'And who will they send? Who's coming?'

Vela blinked again and then his eyes closed. Beth closed the door.

'Did you hear him?' she whispered out on the landing. 'Did you hear what he just said?'

Harry nodded.

The word he used was *hunters*.

THE C-47 SWEPT in low across the flat countryside to the east of Oswestry and touched down at Rednal Aerodrome just before three a.m. in a thunder of reverse thrust and a cloud of fine spray.

Nash peered through the window as the aircraft taxied towards the control tower. Every building was shrouded in darkness. After a minute the C-47 rocked to a halt and Nash saw figures scurrying beneath the fuselage, chocking the undercarriage. As the propellers wound down, someone wedged a small staircase against the door. Ron Chambers got up from his seat and cracked it open.

A cold wind gusted around the aircraft. Nash tugged on his overcoat and angled a felt Fedora over his thinning hair. He stepped out into a fine drizzle.

Ron and Syd stood beneath umbrellas at the bottom of the stairs, their luggage lined up in a neat row at their feet. The welcoming party stood a short distance away, six men and three cars almost lost in the black shadows of the hanger. Nash saw two uniforms amongst them.

'Who's in charge here?'

One of the uniforms stepped forward. 'I'm Chief

Constable Ballard, Shropshire police, and this is Chief Constable Pritchard of the North Wales constabulary. These men are our immediate subordinates.' Ballard motioned to the group behind him.

'My name is Nash, from Whitehall. This is Mister Chambers and Mister Phelan. Mister Chambers is my security officer, and you'll provide him with every assistance, is that clear?'

In the darkness, Nash saw Ballard glower. *A man unused to being woken in the middle of the night and ordered to report to a deserted airfield.*

'Is that clear?' Nash repeated, glaring at Ballard. The policeman nodded and Nash addressed the whole group.

'Gentlemen, I am the senior authority here and will remain so for the duration of this incident. If any of you are unhappy with this arrangement and quietly intend to test my authority, please do so now. That way I can dismantle your career without further ado.'

Nash looked from face to face, his eyes lingering on Ballard. Any traces of rebellion had quickly disappeared from the chief constable's demeanour.

'So it's true then?' Pritchard asked, his resonant Welsh accent cutting through the gloom. 'There's some sort of rocket ship up there in the mountains. Explains all the cloak-and-dagger stuff, right?'

Nash stepped closer. Rain dripped off the peak of Pritchard's service cap. 'That's the first and last time I want to hear that phrase, Chief Constable. Nor do I want to hear words like *spaceship, spacecraft, ufo,* or any such variant in any communication, be it verbal or otherwise. Your officers will hand in their notebooks. They will speak to no one, and that includes each other. Communications will be restricted, and all witness reports will be handled by Mister

Phelan. Do I make myself clear?' Cowed voices mumbled in the darkness. 'Good. Now, what's the situation?'

Pritchard cleared his throat. 'The crash site, Craggan Peak, has been secured. There's only one serviceable track that leads up to the summit and that's been blocked by a local car. There're a couple of hiking paths as well, but I've stationed officers on all of them.'

'And the village? Finnhagel?'

'Sealed off. Telephones are out too. Chief Constable Ballard has a road-block in place down in the valley. The whole mountain is effectively isolated.'

'The crash site, is it visible from anywhere else?'

'No,' confirmed Pritchard. 'The witness who called it in is a local farm manager, knows the area like the back of his hand. He says it's lying in a shallow depression a couple of hundred yards short of the peak.'

'I want files on everyone who's contacted the police, especially those that live closest to the crash site, and I want them before sun up. Clear?' Nash registered the obedient murmurs. He gestured to the three black Ford Zephyrs glistening in the rain. 'I take it one of those is for us.' It wasn't a question.

'Yes,' confirmed Ballard. 'We'll escort you to Oswestry. We've arranged accommodations in the local hotel.'

'We'll be heading straight up to the crash site. We'll need a place to stay close by.'

A voice in the darkness said, 'There's a pub in the village, *The Griffin*. They have lodgings.'

Nash shook his head. 'We'll commandeer something when we get there. Let's get moving, shall we?'

Engines fired up and doors slammed. Phelan got behind the wheel of the trailing Zephyr while Chambers loaded the luggage in the boot. He slid in the back, next to Nash.

'We may need to lean hard on this one, Ron. If the witnesses are right, our Fallen Angel might also have brought a few cherubs with her, and that cannot go public, ever. Once our people have secured the site I want you and Syd to go through the witness statements, find out who saw what. Then we'll talk.'

The former Military Policeman nodded. 'Understood, Mister Nash.'

Through the wiper blades, the cars in front began to pull away. Phelan dropped the Zephyr into gear and followed them, out of the deserted aerodrome and west towards the distant, unseen mountain range.

FALLEN ANGEL

'RITA! WHERE'S THAT BLOODY CAMERA?'

Dougie was in the bedroom, emptying the drawers as fast as his hands would allow. Clothes flew, onto the bed, the floor. He knew he didn't have much time. The police had already driven up to the forest and blocked off the track, but that wouldn't stop him. He'd drive the Land Rover into the field opposite the house, cut across it, up to the stone bluffs that marked the edge of the moor. He'd leave the vehicle near the fence and go the rest of the way on foot. It would be a long slog, a mile or so, all uphill and over some rough terrain, but it would be worth it, Dougie Booth was certain of that. And by the time he got up there the sun would be up. Perfect.

But he needed that camera.

'Rita! Where are you? Where's the bloody camera?'

Rita bustled into the room, wrapped in her dressing gown. She had curlers in her hair and a cigarette in her hand. 'What's all the shouting for? They'll hear you in the village.'

'The camera,' Dougie repeated. 'Where is it?'

Rita frowned, sucking on her cigarette. 'I'm trying to think when we last used it. My cousin's wedding over in Telford, wasn't it?'

Dougie yanked out the bottom drawer and emptied it onto the bed. A china ornament dropped to the floorboards and shattered.

'Dougie, for God's sake—'

The farm manager spun around and grabbed his wife by the shoulders. He shook her hard. Cigarette ash tumbled to the floor. 'Listen to me, you stupid cow! Soon that peak will be crawling with coppers. Before that happens, I need to get up there and take some pictures.'

Rita's voice trembled. 'They're not letting anyone up there, you said. You'll get in trouble.'

Dougie shook her again. 'Think about it, for God's sake! How much d'you think the papers will pay for a picture of a real-life flying saucer? I'll tell you, an absolute bloody fortune. Like winning the pools. Now, where's that camera?'

Rita's eyes shifted towards the window. Dougie heard it too, and his heart sank. He let go of his wife and peered through the curtain. A black car was driving past the house, then its brake lights glowed red in the mist. It turned into the courtyard below.

'Damn it,' Dougie muttered. The opportunity had passed, he knew that now. He waved a hand at the bed. 'Clear this mess up, will you?'

'What about the camera?'

Dougie glared at his wife. He thought about cracking her around the chops, then decided against it and hurried downstairs. When he opened the front door, he saw three men in dark coats climbing out of the Zephyr. Dougie heard a growing rumbling. The next moment, two lorries lumbered past the farm, belching diesel smoke as they headed up the mountain. Dougie glimpsed soldiers sitting in the back, their black striped faces, guns and camouflage jackets, before he lost them in the darkness. Any faint hope he might've had of getting back to the crash site was now well and truly gone.

He turned his attention to the men outside his door. The one wearing a fedora approached and flashed an identification card.

'You're Douglas Booth, yes?' Dougie nodded. 'My name's Nash. You reported a downed aircraft, correct?'

'Nope. I said it was a *flying saucer*. Saw it with my own eyes. It's sitting up there on the peak. From Mars, probably.'

The man took a step closer. 'This is a national security matter, Mister Booth. What you saw is a Russian satellite. We've been tracking its descent for days.'

Dougie snorted. 'And what about the little green men inside it, eh? Are they Russians too?'

The man turned to his companions, then turned back. 'Why don't you tell us exactly what happened?'

Dougie spent five minutes telling them everything he knew. *Better to play along,* he reasoned. When he'd finished, the man in the fedora spoke.

'We're commandeering your Land Rover.'

'What for?'

'We need a suitable vehicle.'

Hope soared. 'I'll take you.' Dougie snatched his coat off the hook behind the door, then stopped short of Nash's leather-gloved hand.

'That won't be necessary, thank you. We just need the vehicle. If you'd be kind enough to look after our car, we'd be much obliged. You'll be reimbursed for your trouble, of course.'

Dougie spied the sleek black Zephyr parked in his muddy courtyard. 'How much?'

'That depends how cooperative you continue to be.'

Dougie fished in his pocket and handed over the keys. 'There you go. She's got a full tank, almost.'

'Thank you, Mister Booth. Much appreciated.'

He watched them squeeze into the front of the Land Rover and turn out of the courtyard. A moment later they were heading up the track. Dougie went back inside and slammed the front door. He sat down in the parlour and filled his pipe, sucking on it until the tobacco burned and sweet smoke drifted on the air. He didn't know much, but he knew one thing for sure. A man only ever got one chance to hit it big in life.

And Dougie Booth's chance had just passed him by.

'What d'you think?' Phelan asked as the jeep climbed higher up the mountain.

Nash wiped condensation from the window. Beyond the rough stone wall, snowy fields were dotted with the white spectres of grazing sheep. The Berwyn Mountains were remote and sparsely populated, something Nash was grateful for. The thought of an event like this taking place in Hyde Park, or some other public spot, gave him nightmares.

'He's the rebellious type,' Chambers warned. 'Not intimidated by authority.'

Nash folded his arms as the jeep bounced and swayed along the track. 'He'll keep his mouth shut for the right price. That, and the threat of prison, of course.'

Another isolated farmhouse took shape from the darkness ahead, set back behind the stone wall and bordered by well-kept gardens. No lights, curtains drawn. Nash watched it until it slipped back into the void.

'Here we go,' Phelan said from behind the wheel.

Up ahead, a forest of pines marched out of the mist towards them. Nash saw the two army lorries parked by the side of the track, and a police car, its helmeted constables chatting to a tall man in camouflage battledress. As Phelan brought the Land Rover to a halt, the military man broke away and approached them. Nash and Chambers climbed out.

Major Frank Hughes cut an intimidating figure, the chiselled face beneath his maroon beret blackened with camouflage cream, the butt of his Browning automatic pistol visible beneath the flap of his holster. Nash knew Hughes and his men would be enough to put the wind up the locals.

'Good to see you, Frank,' Nash said, shaking the soldier's hand.

'You too, Peter.' Hughes smiled at Chambers. 'Big Ron. How are you, old chap?'

'I'm well.' The security officer glanced at Hughes' cap badge. 'Who's this?'

'Staffordshire Regiment, airborne detachment. Should muddy the waters.' Hughes glanced over his shoulder, at the invisible peak far above them. 'So this is it, then? The real thing?'

'We're about to find out.' Nash pointed to the tree-line. 'Set up your check point here, Frank. No one passes it but our people. The recovery team should be here soon, so wave them straight up.'

'Will do.' Hughes cocked a thumb at the lorries jammed with watching soldiers. 'I'll deploy the lads across the mountain, static and roving patrols.'

'Keep it tight and discreet,' Nash told him. 'I don't want

to see anything moving up there apart from us. As usual, Ron has complete authority to act on my behalf, so if you get any political trouble, let him know.'

'Understood.' Hughes turned and circled his finger in the air. Tailgates swung open and soldiers dropped to the ground. Two dozen of them jogged towards the ancient, dry-stone wall, leapt over it and headed out into the darkness. Another soldier hurried towards Hughes, carrying a man-portable radio pack.

'Put it in the Rover,' Hughes told him, pointing to Nash's commandeered vehicle. 'It's been pre-tuned,' he told Nash. 'Here's a list of frequencies.'

Nash jammed it in his pocket. He nodded to the police constables who were watching events with open curiosity. 'Send them back down to Finnhagel, to the police cordon there. That's as far as our uniformed friends go, unless I say otherwise.'

'What about the people who live up here?' Ron asked. 'Can't have them sniffing around.'

'First things first,' Nash said. He slapped Hughes on the shoulder. 'Lock this mountain down tight, Frank.'

'Will do.'

Nash and Chambers climbed back into the Rover. Phelan had kept the engine running, and the cab had warmed up nicely. He jammed the vehicle into gear and headed past the trucks, plunging into the inky void of the forest. Headlights picked out the thickly packed ranks of pine trunks, the occasional startled rabbit bolting into the undergrowth. They climbed towards the peak in silence, and Nash knew that each of them was preparing themselves for what they were about to see. Unless Booth's witness account was a complete fabrication. Something told Nash it wasn't, and his heart beat fast in anticipation. This was everything he'd worked for, everything he'd dreamed about. In a few minutes, he would know.

The forest yielded to a landscape of shifting mist and barren, snow-crusted moorland. They left the Land Rover on the track and Nash led his team out across empty, sloping ground. The mist wrapped itself around them like a damp cloak, smothering the beams of their torches. The thick carpet of snow-capped ferns soaked his trousers, though Nash barely felt it. He trod carefully as the ground sloped away to his right, the mist thickening as they moved parallel to the peak above them. Visibility dropped to less than ten yards. Nash slowed his pace, his torch sweeping left and right. He took another three or four steps then stopped. Chambers walked into him.

'Sorry, Mister Nash—'

Nash held up his hand for silence. He directed his torch beam above them.

'Jesus Christ,' he heard Phelan whisper.

Over their heads, the tail of the craft jutted out of the mist. It was black and rudderless, with a wide vent that Nash assumed was an exhaust port. He stared up at it, transfixed. It was magnificent, and it took his breath away. It filled him with a sudden urge to yell his joy across the mountain, but the emotion was fleeting. He had a job to do.

Phelan was already clicking away with his camera, the flash pulsing every couple of seconds. Chambers pointed to the scar of churned mud and vegetation that stretched back into the mist. 'Looks like it hit the slope somewhere down there.'

'Not a crash then,' Nash observed. 'More like a crash landing.'

'Let's check the perimeter. Keep your eyes open.'

Nash led them up the slope, keeping the craft on his

right, it's glass-like black body splattered with mud and vegetation. All Nash could hear was their breathing as they stamped through thick ferns. The surrounding moor was silent, the mist impenetrable, as if Mother Nature herself intended to keep their secret safe. Nash knew that wouldn't last long. Speed was vital now.

They rounded the nose of the craft, now buried in a mound of dirt and mud, and down the other side. Nash had a better idea of its size and shape now, and it reminded him of an airship, except its flanks were smooth and seamless. As they headed back down the slope, Chambers pointed.

'Look.'

Nash saw it too, an open hatch, low to the ground, the surrounding ferns crushed to sticky mud. A faint blue light glowed from inside. Nash reached inside his coat and drew his firearm. Chambers already had his clenched in his big hand. They approached warily while Phelan kept his distance, still taking pictures.

'Careful, gents,' the younger man urged.

Nash heard the tremble in his voice. None of them knew what lay beyond. Chambers was squatting down beside the hatch, peering inside.

'Someone's beat us to it.'

A rush of panic gripped Nash. He knelt down next to Chambers and peered inside, following the sweep of his torch beam. Just inside the hatch there was mud, and several handprints. Beyond the hatch was a crawlspace, narrow but large enough for him to squeeze through. He stood up, yanked a surgical mask from his pocket, and shook off his overcoat.

'I'm going inside.'

'That's against protocol,' Chambers warned him.

'If there's someone in there, I want to know who it is. If I'm not back in five minutes, do not follow me, is that clear?'

'Watch your step,' Chambers cautioned. 'Shout if you need me.'

With a torch in one hand and a gun in the other, Nash crawled inside the space. It was about five feet long, its walls smooth to the touch and free of welds or rivets. The tunnel emptied into a chamber on the other side, and Nash got to his feet. There was a gap in the wall ahead, like a partially shut sliding door. Nash approached it, his gun held low, the torch sweeping ahead. Nothing moved, the craft silent inside. It was warmer too, and dry, and something tainted the air with an odour that he couldn't place. He stepped through the sliding door, aimed his torch at the rubber-like tiles on the floor. More mud. More evidence that someone had been inside. He waved his torch around the compact room, glimpsing something pale. The beam settled. Nash's heart leapt inside his chest.

Bodies.

Three of them, slumped in their seats. Nash holstered his firearm, his mouth dry, his heart pounding, his mask inflating and deflating. The beings were strapped into chairs, two behind two, the rear chairs set higher and separated from each other by some sort of control console. They were all facing forward, towards the crumpled nose, and it was clear the impact had caused significant damage to the instrumentation panels that appeared to be made of glass. Many of them were cracked or shattered completely. *It's the cockpit,* Nash realised. Which meant he was looking at the crew.

He took a step closer to the nearest body. *An alien being, from another world, another universe—my God!* Despite his training, despite the conditioning and the

64

psychological preparation, Nash's jaw dropped open. His limbs felt weak and hollow. The being was slumped in its seat, its head lolling on its chest. It was small, its head larger and out of proportion to the rest of its body. Its eyes were set wider on its head and were black, with no visible pupils. Nash reached out with a gloved hand and lifted the arm of the creature. It had a thumb but only three fingers, and they hung lifeless. He placed two of his own fingers on the exposed neck and felt for a pulse. He had little chance of finding one through his gloves, but he wouldn't risk contamination. *Nothing.* If the being had a heart, it wasn't beating.

Nash knew he had to leave. He'd already broken every rule in the book. Insubordination was a concept as alien as the craft he was standing in, but confronted with the opportunity, Nash had been powerless to resist. He took one last look around and turned back towards the sliding door. Thirty seconds later he was back outside, walking away from the craft, dragging the surgical mask down around his neck. His breath fogged on the cold air, his heart still hammering.

'Mister Nash, are you okay?' Chambers stood a few feet away, his brow furrowed, his eyes flicking towards the craft.

'You're right, Ron, someone was in there. There's something else inside too.' He paused for a moment, then said, 'Casualties.'

Phelan stumbled through the ferns towards them. 'Did I hear you right, Mister Nash? There're bodies in there?'

Nash nodded. 'Three of them. The ship's crew, by the look of it. And definitely not from here.' He took a deep breath to slow his heart rate and gather his thoughts. 'Okay, this is a confirmed *Fallen Angel*. Syd, get back to the jeep and get on the radio. Tell Frank we need ropes and tarpaulins up here fast. We need to get it covered up before the wind picks up and the whole bloody world sees it. Get an ETA on that recovery team too, and put a call in to Condor. Tell them this is the real thing. Move!'

He watched Phelan bolt into the mist. Then he turned to Chambers, who stood watching him, gun in hand, up to his knees in snow and ferns. The plea was clear in his eyes. Nash cocked his head.

'Go, take a look. Tell me I'm not seeing things. And be quick about it.'

Ron Chambers holstered his pistol and ran back towards the hatch.

RING OF STEEL

Daylight streamed through a thin crack in the curtains. Harry stirred, then opened his eyes. He'd slept in, which was unusual for him. He sat up and saw blood on his pillow. Not a lot of blood, but enough to concern him.

He rolled out of bed, careful not to wake a sleeping Beth. He wrapped a dressing gown over his pyjamas and padded into the bathroom next door. He looked in the mirror; his thick dark hair was a mess, and he rubbed at the shadow of stubble around his jaw. He poked a finger in his ear and felt a thin crust. He turned his head; dried blood crusted his ear and lobe. A faint headache thumped behind his eyeballs too. Not good.

A few handfuls of tepid water helped to blow off some cobwebs. He dressed in trousers, a checked shirt and a thick green jumper. Downstairs in the kitchen he filled the kettle and put it on the stove. He marched into the dining room and pulled back the curtains. The police car that had raced past the house last night was no longer there. In its place, two army lorries, and soldiers with guns and blackened faces.

He headed back upstairs. He'd check on Vela first, then wake Charlie, get him dressed and fed. He wasn't sure about school. Halfway up the stairs he heard his son's muffled laughter. He opened the boy's bedroom door and his heart skipped a beat.

The laughter was coming from the spare bedroom.

Harry went to the door and flung it open, snapping on the light. Charlie was in his pyjamas, sat on the rug by the bed. He turned and smiled.

'Hello, Dad.'

Vela sat upright, his back against a pillow, the eiderdown wrapped around his narrow shoulders. His eyes blinked as Harry closed the door behind him.

'Everything okay in here?'

'Vela was telling me about the wildlife on his planet. Did you know they have an animal just like a monkey, but instead of two arms it has four? And birds the size of sheep!'

'No, I didn't know that, Son. Sounds amazing.' While he spoke his eyes never left Vela. Charlie seemed completely at ease, and Harry was wondering how that had happened. His son was an introvert, a challenge for every teacher who'd ever taught him, yet a strange-looking visitor didn't seem to upset him at all.

'How are you feeling?'

Harry frowned. 'What's that, Son?'

'Vela wants to know how you're feeling.'

A bemused Harry said, 'I'm okay. A little groggy actually.'

Charlie touched the side of his own head. 'He says the pressure here will pass. It's a side effect of the telepathy.'

Harry dropped to the rug and inspected Charlie's ears. All clear. He glared at Vela. 'If this telepathy stuff is dangerous, I need you to stop doing it to my son.'

Charlie smiled. 'Vela says your brain isn't very advanced, Dad. Mine is different. I won't come to any harm.'

'Different how?' Harry cupped his son's face. The boy's eyes were clear and bright, his cheeks a healthy pink. There didn't seem to be anything wrong with him at all. 'How d'you feel, Son?'

'I'm fine. Vela said you shouldn't concern yourself.'

'Easy for him to say.'

'Did you see the soldiers, Dad?'

'Yes.'

'They've come to take Vela away with them. You won't let them, will you?'

Harry directed his answer at Vela. 'I'm not sure I could stop them.'

'They want his ship too.'

Harry stood up and pulled a chair next to the bed. Vela blinked as Harry spoke to him.

'What happened up there? The crash, I mean?'

Charlie was watching Vela and nodding. Then he turned to Harry. 'He says the anti-matter displacement drive failed. A complete core failure. It happens, he says.'

Harry winced. 'A what?'

Charlie smiled. 'They broke down.'

He stared at his son. It was so strange to hear him talking like that, using words that he neither knew nor understood. Harry felt a faint stirring of anger; his boy was being used as some sort of transmitter. He felt Charlie's hand squeeze his fingers.

'Vela says he understands your concern, but I'm not in any physical danger. He says my brain is wired differently. That I can't come to any harm.'

'You're sure?' Harry asked Vela. 'You promise me he won't be harmed? In any way?'

Vela nodded his hairless head.

'You have his word,' Charlie told him.

Harry nodded too. 'Okay, then.' His gut instinct told him that their visitor meant none of them any harm. It was the same feeling he had that night over Germany, when the ship had emerged from the cloud bank and flew alongside them. No threat, no danger. Harry had always trusted his instincts. He had to trust them again.

'So, what's this *port* thing you mentioned last night?'

'It's a *portal*,' Charlie corrected. 'He says it's a gateway, a safe point of passage where their ships can come and go without attracting attention. There's one not too far away.'

'Where does this portal lead to?'

Vela pointed to the ceiling.

'Off-world,' Charlie told him.

Harry stared at them both. 'You've lost me.'

'Space, Dad. Where d'you think?'

There was a soft knock at the door and Beth entered, wrapped in a dressing gown. She'd tied her long blonde hair up but her eyes were still puffy. Eyes that widened when she saw Charlie.

'He's fine,' Harry said, getting to his feet. 'They met before I got up. How are you?'

'I've lost a little blood—'

'From your ears, yes? And you've probably got a headache too. It's a side effect of the telepathy. Vela's communicating through Charlie now.' Beth opened her mouth to speak but Harry beat her to it. 'Vela says he won't come to any harm. I believe him, Beth. Charlie's fine. Right, Son?'

They both looked down at the boy at their feet. Charlie

beamed up at them, his thumbs in the air. 'Vela said I was special.'

Beth nodded, her eyes suddenly moist. 'That's right, that's exactly what you are.' She looked at Vela. 'He's all we've got. Please don't hurt him.'

Vela shook his head.

'All he wants to do is to leave,' Charlie told her. 'Via the portal. Off-world.'

Harry saw the worry creasing Beth's face and said, 'It's weird, I know, but in a good way.'

'I hope so.' Beth stood by the bed and pointed at Vela's legs. 'May I?'

Vela nodded permission. Beth unwrapped the bandages and inspected his injuries. She held up one of the shrivelled cabbage leaves to the overhead light. 'The moisture has been sucked out of this completely.'

'Not just moisture,' Charlie told her. 'Micro and macro-nutrients, complex carbohydrates, base ionic compounds. Further absorption is essential for regrowth.'

Beth and Harry stared at their son. 'This will take some getting used to,' she realised. She turned back to Vela's wounds and squinted. She stepped past Harry. 'We need some light in here—'

Before Harry could protest, Beth was yanking back the curtains. Then she froze. 'Harry, there's a man looking through our window.'

He hurried to her side. A big man, hatless, with short hair and a long dark overcoat, had his hands cupped against the kitchen window below. Harry pulled Beth away and dragged the curtains closed.

'Stay here and keep quiet.' He took the stairs two at a time and yanked open the front door. Two men in black suits and overcoats waited on the damp flagstones outside.

One of them was the big fella, a rough-looking type with a flat nose and cauliflower ears. The nosy one. Harry addressed him first.

'You were trespassing. Do it again and I'll call the police.'

The man stared at Harry, neither friendly nor otherwise. He didn't even blink.

'You must excuse Mister Chambers. He's a curious soul. The policeman's blood in his veins, no doubt.'

The man who spoke wore a black fedora above a chiselled jaw and a pencil-thin moustache. His dark blue tie was perfectly knotted, his black suit and overcoat immaculate. Except for his trousers and shoes, which were wet and caked with mud. Likewise, his companion. Harry knew where they'd just come from.

'What do you want?' Harry asked him.

'My name is Nash,' the man said, flashing his credentials. 'We're investigating the incident that occurred here last night.'

Harry pointed. 'You're *Air Ministry*. Is that what it was? A plane crash?'

Nash stared from beneath his brim. 'You should know, Mister Wakefield. You've been up there.'

Dougie. Big bloody mouth. Harry shook his head. 'Part of the way, but I stopped short. Couldn't see much through the trees. Thought it might be dangerous, so I waited for the authorities.'

Harry looked past Nash to a younger, black-suited man standing by the gate. He had a clear complexion, with dark hair combed back off a high forehead. He had a large, angular nose, and he was talking to a police officer who handed him a file.

'We need two things,' Nash continued. 'First, a statement and second, we'll need you to vacate your property.' He snapped his arm out and glanced at his watch. 'You've got an hour to pack a few essentials. I've made arrangements for you to stay down in the village. *The Griffin,* I believe it's called. Full board, for the duration.'

Harry felt the blood rushing to his cheeks. He struggled to keep his voice even. 'That's out of the question. This is a working farm. I need to be here, as does my farm manager, Dougie Booth. He's further down the hill.'

'Everything beyond the village is now a restricted area, however you'll be allowed back onto your land this afternoon. Essential duties only,' Nash told him. 'For the rest of the time you'll remain in the village.'

'That's just not practical—'

Nash tapped his watch. 'One hour,' he repeated in a voice that dared Harry to argue the point.

Harry closed the door. As his hand reached for the bolt, he saw his fingers were shaking.

EVICTION

'HE's LYING,' Chambers said as they climbed back into the Land Rover.

'Maybe.'

Nash was reading the file that Syd had given him. It was thin, a few pages of names and addresses from the national census in sixty-one, and a separate list of people who'd contacted the police. Harry Wakefield was an ex-serviceman. Which meant he'd have a file.

'Evacuate every other house on the mountain. Let's get all our eggs in one basket. Any news on the recovery transport?'

'They'll be here within the hour. And I just got word from Condor. The American just landed at Rednal Aerodrome. He'll be right behind the convoy.'

'Where's the farmhand?'

'Solitary confinement in Oswestry nick,' Chambers told him. 'Hughes has sent a couple of his men down to watch him. As soon as the transport arrives, he'll be transferred to RAF Machrihanish.'

'Good work. We'll wait for the transport to get here,

then we'll set ourselves up in Wakefield's place. Hopefully, we'll all be back at Machrihanish in a couple of days.'

HARRY WENT to the dining-room window and peered outside. Nash and his goons were climbing into the Land Rover. He waited until the vehicle had disappeared into the mist before heading back upstairs.

He found Beth, Charlie and Vela sitting in darkness. Beth got to her feet as Harry closed the door.

'Who were they?'

'Air Ministry, but they felt more like intelligence types to me.'

'They know about the ship. One of them went inside,' Charlie explained.

Harry frowned. 'How can he know that?'

Charlie smiled. 'Watch...'

Vela raised his arm and pointed to the fireplace at the end of the bed. The hair on Harry's neck stood up as a large square of light shimmered in the air between the bed and the fireplace. It was like a poor TV signal, full of snow and static, and then it cleared and Harry saw Nash, stood in some kind of doorway. He had a mask over his nose and mouth and a gun in his hand. His eyes were wide as his head swivelled around.

'My God, that's amazing,' Beth whispered. 'It's like watching television.'

Harry stared at the shimmering square of moving images. 'That's Nash, the bloke at the door a minute ago. He's commandeering this house.'

Beth's head snapped around. 'He what?'

'Just wait, Beth.' He turned to Vela and said, 'What are we looking at here?'

'The inside of his ship,' Charlie told him. 'Vela's channelling the energy from his friend's expired body. He can utilise his visual receptors.'

Beth held her hands over her mouth. 'Oh my God, he's looking through his dead friend's eyes,' she realised.

The image crackled and the square of light faded to nothing. Harry ran his hand through the air where only a moment ago it hovered brightly. 'How did you do that?'

Vela tilted his head and formed what looked like a smile. It was Charlie who explained.

'He says our world is alive with energy. He says it's everywhere, invisible and untapped.' Charlie smiled and said, 'The air in this room has enough stored energy to power the whole of London for months on end. That's amazing, right Mum?'

Beth's lower lip trembled. She dropped to her knees and wrapped her arms around her son. 'Yes, Charlie. It really is.' Harry watched her run her hands over his head, checking his eyes, his ears. Examining him.

'He gave us his word,' Harry told her. 'I believe him.'

'I can't help it.'

'He's fine. But we've got less than an hour to leave this house.'

Beth got to her feet. 'We can't do that, Harry.'

'We've no choice. We'll be staying at *The Griffin* in the meantime.'

'No,' Beth barked. 'We're not going anywhere.'

'We have to!' Harry hissed. 'This Nash person, he's from the government, and they're not messing around. We don't have a choice.'

'What about Vela?' she asked.

'We take him with us.'

'How do we—'

'I don't know. Look, the clock's ticking. Pack a few things for you and Charlie. I'll bring the Land Rover around the back. We'll work it out, somehow.'

Corporal Billy Stone, erstwhile of the Royal Electrical and Mechanical Engineers, brought the massive Antar Mark Three tank transporter down another gear as he slowed for the turning ahead. He checked his mirrors and saw the string of headlights behind him stretching far into the distance. He imagined the drivers of those vehicles cursing the slow-moving convoy in front of them, but Billy didn't care because he was too excited. For the last three years he'd been a member of the army's Special Projects Team, and now, finally, they'd deployed. And this time it wasn't an exercise.

Police cars blocked the road ahead of him and Billy had to swing the Antar out wide to get his semi-trailer around the tight left-hander. The convoy had covered the one-hundred and forty-eight miles from RAF Alconbury as fast as it could, hoping they'd get off the main roads before sunrise, but that had proved impossible because of the Antar's low speed. Still, they were here now, and the Berwyn Mountains rose ahead of them, a snow-capped landscape of hills, peaks and valleys beneath an oppressive crown of dark clouds. Billy's windshield wipers were already beating off a fine drizzle that fell in silvery sheets across the road ahead.

Billy's crew-mate, Lance Corporal Ernie Fossey, flipped through his map cards until he found the one marked with the crash site. 'Going to be a tight squeeze, Billy.'

'Soft ground too,' Billy added, gunning the powerful engine as he cranked the Antar up a gear.

Ernie fished in his tunic and pulled out a crumpled pack of cigarettes. He lit two and handed one to Billy. 'So this is it, then. The real thing.'

'I wouldn't dwell on it too much,' Billy warned, puffing on his smoke. 'Let's just keep our heads down and do our jobs. Unless you want to go back to your old unit?'

Ernie snorted. 'No chance.' Neither of them wanted to return to the repetitive tedium of barrack life.

'That's what I thought,' Billy grinned, cigarette smoke leaking through his teeth. 'Makes you wonder though, eh? What did that yank call 'em? *Interstellar craft?*'

'Something like that.'

'And *entities.* That's the little blokes driving 'em.'

'I wonder what they call us?' Ernie mused. 'Ignorant apes, I suppose.'

Billy wagged a finger. 'And that's exactly what we're gonna be. See nothing, hear nothing, say nothing. Just like them three monkeys.'

A police car raced past them on the other side of the road, its blue light flashing. A path was being cleared ahead of them, all the way to the crash site. Despite the Yank's words of warning, Billy was quietly looking forward to getting there. To seeing it. To touching it. A machine from another world. *Amazing.*

The Antar's engine roared as the road took them higher and deeper into the dark, barren mountain range.

A POLICEMAN STEPPED out into the road and raised his hand. Harry pumped the brakes and crunched the gears as he brought the Land Rover to a stop just outside Finnhagel.

'This is crazy,' Beth whispered. 'He'll find him.'

'Quiet.' Harry opened his window and smiled. 'Morning constable.'

The policeman was wearing a rain slicker over his uniform. Water dripped off the rim of his helmet. 'Can I help you folks?'

He looked past Harry and inspected the interior of the Land Rover. Beth forced a smile. Charlie grinned from the rear compartment, bundled in a dark anorak and hat, his wellington boots propped on a large pile of hessian.

'Our house has been commandeered,' Harry explained. 'Lodgings have been organised at *The Griffin*.'

The policeman nodded. 'They did tell me to expect some traffic.' He pointed down the hill towards the high street. 'On you go, sir.'

Harry released the handbrake, and a minute later he was pulling into the pub car park, which was pretty busy. Beth and Charlie got out as Harry reversed the Rover into a corner space, tight against the stone wall.

'You just rest,' he muttered over his shoulder. There was no response in his head, no movement beneath the pile of black hessian behind him. Harry hooked up a curtain of material across the back seats and climbed out, locking the vehicle.

'Is he going to be okay?' Beth asked Charlie.

The boy nodded. 'He's sleeping now, conserving his energy. The most important thing is getting him to the portal.'

'And he told you where we find this portal?' Harry asked his son.

'It's eighty miles away. He doesn't have long.'

Beth frowned. 'What do you mean?'

'Harry?'

79

Gavin Souter stood at the back door of the pub, his hands in his pockets.

'Come on,' he whispered to Beth and Charlie. 'And remember, not a word about anything.'

They picked up their bags and crossed the car park. Souter glanced at the suitcases in their hands. 'More refugees,' he chuckled.

'They've commandeered the house,' Harry explained. 'They said arrangements had been made to stay here.'

Souter nodded. 'You're not the only ones, but don't worry, Meg will sort you out. Got you something cosy upstairs.'

Fifteen minutes later they were settling into a three-bed family room at the back of the pub. It overlooked the car park, which was a bonus, and Harry watched the Land Rover for a few moments. 'Charlie, what did you mean, *he doesn't have long?*'

The boy frowned beneath his pudding-bowl haircut. 'I can't remember. Something to do with the air. What's in it. *Night*, something. A funny word.'

'Nitrogen,' Beth said.

Charlie smiled. 'That's it, Mum! Nitrogen!'

'Shh,' Harry whispered, stroking his son's hair. 'What about it?'

'Vela says there's too much of it. It's making him ill. That's why he has to get to the portal.'

Harry heard the crunch of gravel and saw another vehicle pulling into the car park, a shiny black Zephyr. It surprised him to see Dougie and Rita clamber out and head towards the pub, overnight bags in hand.

'Dougie and Rita are here,' Harry observed.

Beth came and stood by his side. 'What're we going to

do? We can't just hang around here, not if Vela's sick. We have to get off the mountain.'

'Gavin says there's a roadblock on the way out of the village. They're not letting anyone leave. Security reasons, they say.'

'They can't do that.'

'D'you want to take the risk?'

There was a gentle tap on the door. Harry opened it. Meg was outside, dolled up in a red satin shirt and matching lipstick.

'Hello, Harry. You're all settled in okay, then?'

'Fine, thanks Meg.'

'I'm serving lunch downstairs at noon. Nothing special, just soup and sandwiches. Thought it might be a good idea to have everyone eat together, you know, community spirit and all that. Just like the war years.'

'Sounds fine.'

'See you in a bit, then.'

Harry closed the door. He sat down on his bed and gathered Beth and Charlie close to him. 'We'll have lunch, act normal. Afterwards I'll go see that Nash fella, tell him we're going to stay at your mum's.' Harry smoothed Charlie's hair. 'And remember, Son, no talk about Vela or anything like that, okay? That's our secret.'

Charlie looked up and smiled.

'Okay, Dad.'

PUB FIGHT

It was the first time Harry had seen *The Griffin* packed with people.

He avoided the public bar, thick with farmers and curious villagers, and guided Beth and Charlie into a corner table in the saloon bar that doubled as a restaurant. A fire roared in the grate and the room hummed with chatter. Harry and Beth nodded a few *hellos* and a pimple-faced kitchen-hand served them bowls of Scotch broth, chicken salad sandwiches and fresh bread and butter. It was good too. Yet as Harry took another mouthful of food, he was troubled by a stab of guilt. Vela was lying in the back of his Land Rover, wrapped up against the cold in a sleeping bag and covered with layers of hessian. He was alone, far from home, and surrounded by primitive beings. Harry had no idea how he must be feeling. Even Charlie seemed sad, his head bowed as he spooned broth into his mouth.

'Are you alright, Son?'

Charlie looked up at him. 'We'll get him to the portal, won't we?'

'A *portal*? What the bloody hell's that, then?'

Harry turned to see Dougie hovering by their table. His words were sharp, his eyes narrow, his cheeks flushed red. Dougie was pissed off, and his voice carried. Heads turned their way; policemen, grabbing a bite to eat, displaced families from the mountain, local villagers. And across the room, four smart-suited men with hard faces. *More government people,* Harry wondered, but their clothes were a little flashier, their demeanour a little less formal. The room watched and listened.

'Mind your language in front of the boy, Dougie.'

The farm manager scowled and sat down. People looked away, started chatting again. Dougie slapped his cap on the table. 'Kicked you out too, did they?'

Harry jerked a thumb at the window. 'What's with the car?'

'Those blokes from the Ministry have borrowed my jeep.'

Harry leaned a little closer. 'Listen, we need to talk. I'm going back to Derbyshire for a couple of days. I'll need you and the boys to look after the farm while I'm gone.'

'We're a man down,' Dougie grumbled. 'They took Colin away. He's down at the station in Oswestry.'

'Why?' Beth asked.

'Why d'you think?' Dougie shot back, his voice rising. 'He went inside that thing. Saw all them Martians.'

'Can I have everyone's attention, please?'

Heads turned towards the bar. Nash and his goons had entered the pub, cutting a swathe through the throng of patrons. Nash didn't take his hat off, nor did he remove his hands from his pockets. When he spoke, it was clear and with authority, his head swivelling around the room.

'There'll be no more talk of Martians, or spaceships, or any such nonsense.'

'What's up there, then?' a voice asked from the back of the room.

'An experimental military aircraft,' Nash explained, 'so this is now a government matter of the utmost secrecy. That's why the army are here and why we've had to cut off the telephones. If someone talks, and our enemies find out, we could have Soviet spies crawling all over this mountain, and we don't want to jeopardise the country's security, do we?'

'My wife has a hospital appointment in Wrexham tomorrow,' a voice said.

'No one can leave the area, not until we've secured the aircraft.'

'That's no bloody aircraft.'

It was Dougie's voice that cut through the compliant murmurs. Harry watched Nash's face as the farm manager addressed the whole pub.

'You all know me. You know I speak plainly, so let me put your minds at rest—that's no *experimental aircraft* up there on the peak. It's a bloody big spaceship. I seen it with my own eyes, stood right up against it, I did. Young Colin Hargreaves, he went inside the thing, saw funny little creatures in there. That's why they've taken him away, because they don't want any of us to know. That's why the phones don't work. They don't want us telling anyone. Nothing to do with the bloody Russians.'

Nash held up a hand to silence the excited jabbering.

'Quiet down, ladies and gentlemen.' The noise died away, and the room refocused on the man from the ministry. 'Thank you. Now, Colin Hargreaves is in isolation in Oswestry awaiting a medical examination because of his potential exposure to radiation—'

Worried voices drowned out Nash's words. He held up

his hand again, and the voices faded to silence.

'The *creatures* that Mister Hargreaves thinks he saw were in fact pigs, dressed in pressure suits and strapped into the aircraft's seats. This is how our scientists measure the effects of supersonic flight on the human body—'

'Flying pigs?' Dougie's cackle cut across the room. 'Let me tell you something, Mister Nash. Young Colin is a farmhand, and a bloody good one. He looks after a couple of dozen pigs up there on the farm, so if you think he can't recognise one when he sees it, you've lost your marbles.'

A wave of rebellious murmurs rippled around the pub. Harry watched Nash. His face boiled, as did those of his companions. They'd lost the room to Dougie, and the farm manager knew it.

'Flying pigs, my arse,' he guffawed, and now others laughed too. Nash looked fit to burst.

The pub began to shake —

Glasses rattled, and even Dougie's triumphant smile slipped from his face. The rumbling grew louder, and the pub darkened. Harry watched Nash and his goons head outside, allowing a throaty roar to fill *The Griffin*.

Harry saw the police cars first, their blue lights blinking through the windows, then the lorries followed, the biggest ones that Harry had ever seen.

'Wait here,' he told Beth, and pushed his way out onto the pavement with a dozen others. It was a tank transporter, Harry saw, green and slick with rain, and towing a long flat trailer. Behind it was another huge lorry, this one with a giant winch and rolls of steel cable on its flat-bed. Another two, smaller trucks followed, each one filled with camouflage-painted soldiers, then more police cars. The convoy rumbled past the pub and up towards the end of the high street. No one had to guess where it was going.

As people filed back inside, Harry lingered. He saw Nash and his men pile into Dougie's jeep and head after the convoy.

A recovery team, he knew. They were taking Vela's ship away.

Back in the pub, Dougie was still holding court.

'Don't listen to them government people,' he was telling everyone. 'They're lying. If they want us to keep quiet about this, it'll cost 'em. London's got millions of pounds stashed away in their fancy banks. About time they put their hands in their pockets and spread that money around a little. For communities that need it. Like ours.'

'Tell 'em, Dougie,' a voice shouted from the public bar.

'They've shafted us for too long,' said another.

'Too bloody right,' Dougie said, thumping his table. 'Leave it to me. I'll speak to that fella, let him know what's what.'

Beth leaned into Harry's ear. 'He's really stirring it up.'

'That Nash bloke didn't look too happy,' Harry agreed, watching Dougie retake his seat.

'What're we going to do?'

'I don't know.'

'We can't stay,' Charlie told them.

Harry and Beth swapped looks. 'Before we do anything, I need to get up to the farm, sort out the feed, repair that fence up in the northern field. I can't expect Dougie to do everything.'

'What about Vela?' Beth whispered.

'He's resting,' Charlie told them. 'He'll tell me when he wakes.'

'Okay. You two go back to the room. I'll scrounge a lift with Dougie.'

· · ·

BILLY STONE GUNNED the Antar's engine, belching diesel from its exhaust stack as the rig finally cleared the trees. Up here, towards the peak, the ground was wide open, which made a nice change. For the last thirty minutes Billy had coaxed the Antar up the track, clipping stone walls and dragging barbed wire fences out of the ground. Then they'd reached the forest, where the roar of the Antar's mighty engine had scattered most of God's creatures in all directions. More trees had been clipped, more banks inadvertently widened by the Antar's thick bumpers, then the trees had thinned as daylight beckoned ahead. Billy had to focus real hard to keep the rig centred on the track, but Ernie was giving him a running commentary of what he could see. It didn't really matter though—they'd both be able to see the flying machine soon enough.

So it was a disappointment when the crash site offered them nothing more than a huge tarpaulin-covered mound just below the peak. It was like someone had erected a giant, bulging tent on the hillside, its sides pinned to the earth with metal stakes. Still, Billy wasn't too worried. The thing had to be transported out of there, and Billy and Ernie would supervise the loading. Soon they would be up close and personal, and that meant there would be plenty of time to get eyes on the most amazing thing he'd ever see in his whole life.

PHELAN BROUGHT the jeep to a halt behind the last troop truck and they clambered out. Nash led the way past the trucks where soldiers were manhandling dozens of railway sleepers and carrying them on to the moor. Nash gave the squaddies a wide berth and headed out towards the ship, now draped in layers of dirty, oily tarpaulins. He snapped the collars of his overcoat up as a chill wind moaned across the moor and up towards the peak, pushing a fine, persistent sleet. He wondered how many more degrees the temperature would have to drop before it turned to snow.

Hughes stamped through the ferns towards them. 'Morning,' he greeted.

'Did you get a weather update?' Nash asked him.

Hughes grimaced. 'Doesn't look good. There's a front pushing down from Scotland. We're in for some snow. We've got twenty-four hours max before this place gets a big dump.'

'You can feel it in the air,' Nash agreed. He pointed to the soldiers out on the track. They were piling up railway sleepers as they hurried back and forwards to the lorries. 'Start getting that track laid and then speak to Corporal Stone. He's in charge of the physical recovery, so give him what he needs.'

Hughes doubled away towards the track. Nash led Phelan and Chambers around the craft. It looked rather sad now, wrapped as it was in fifty canvas sheets, like Gulliver tied to the ground by the people of Lilliput. He ducked underneath and saw that the hatch was still open, the interior partially protected from the elements by the tarps, and he wondered if the damp climate would cause any lasting damage inside the craft.

'We need to get that hatch sealed somehow,' Nash observed. 'Especially for the journey.'

'What about the Yank?' Chambers asked. 'We'll need his authority.'

'He should be here any minute. Let's be courteous and professional, okay? Give him what he needs.' Nash looked up at the ship, his hands thrust deep into his pockets. 'After all, he's done this before.'

DEBT OF DISHONOUR

THE WIND GUSTED, driving sleet across the field in cold sheets. Harry grabbed a bale of wire and gave the loose end to Dougie, who ran it out along the length of the damaged fence. Harry snipped it clean, and together they secured it to the new fence posts. In the grey cloud somewhere above them, the rumble of diesel engines drifted across the mountainside.

'Sounds like they're pretty busy up there,' Harry observed, twisting the wire with pliers and checking the tension. Dougie didn't answer him. 'Everything alright over there?' Harry raised his voice a little. Dougie said nothing, still hunched over a fence post, fiddling with the wires. 'Dougie?'

The farm manager walked past him and threw his tools in the back of the tractor trailer. Harry felt his temper rising. He marched over to the trailer.

'If you've got something to say, Dougie, I suggest you get it off your chest instead of sulking like a baby.'

Dougie wiped his hands on his battered jacket and glared at Harry. 'Who d'you think you are, talking to me like that? If it wasn't for me, this farm would be finished. You'd be broke. All of you.'

'And you'd be out of a job,' Harry countered.

Dougie's cackle was dry and humourless. 'I've been working these hills for forty years, man and boy. I know every farm and family for ten miles in any direction. I'm respected, valued. No one knows you, Harry bloody Wakefield, or your missus. You couldn't tell the difference between a ram and a ewe when you first showed up, and things ain't improved much since then either. You've fallen on your feet though, that's a fact, while the rest of us have been ignored. Cast by the bloody wayside.'

Dougie's face was crimson, his chest heaving.

'So that's what this is about,' Harry realised. He swept an arm around the mountainside. 'We didn't ask for this, you know. It came out of the blue, but we were grateful for the opportunity. We're trying to make a go of it, do the best we can, do right by you and Rita—'

'He left us nothing!' Dougie yelled. 'Blood, sweat and tears I gave that man. Thirty years' service on this farm alone. And what've I got to show for it? Nothing! That's what!'

'Calm down, for Chrissakes.'

'Don't tell me to calm down!' Dougie snapped back. Then his eyes narrowed, his finger pointing up towards the peak. 'You took something from that space ship, didn't you?'

Harry swallowed. 'What're you talking about?'

'Last night. You were driving as if the devil himself was chasing ya. Told me to get out of the way, remember? There was something on your front seat. I saw it. What was it?'

'I don't know what you're talking about.'

'Liar! You got yourself a little souvenir, didn't ya?

Gonna sell it to the papers, I bet. Make yourself a tidy sum. As if you ain't had enough luck already.'

Harry heard the rattle of equipment behind him and saw a line of soldiers patrolling the field on the other side of the fence. Harry stared at them as they passed, but no one uttered a word. A few moments later they had moved out of sight. Harry took a deep breath. The military interruption had de-escalated tensions a little, and Harry was glad of it. Things felt like they were about to get out of hand.

'C'mon, we've got work to do.'

Harry threw his tools into the trailer and climbed up into the tractor cab. The engine rattled into life, and he watched a sullen Dougie stand motionless in the field, deep in thought. Like he was trying to decide something. Then he stamped around the tractor and climbed in next to Harry.

'We'll drop feed in the southern field then loop around and do the same in the eastern meadow. After that we'll head back to the village, get a cup of tea.'

Dougie didn't answer. Instead, he stared out of the window as the tractor bounced across the field and back towards the track.

BETH WAS SITTING on the bed, a pillow propped against the headboard as she read a book. It was H.G. Wells' *The Time Machine,* and she'd plucked it from the shelf as she'd left the house. Why she chose a science-fiction book over one of her usual romance novels, she didn't know. Or perhaps she did.

Charlie was on his own bed, drawing pictures with his coloured crayons. Beth stopped reading and watched him for a moment. Charlie was quiet, subdued almost, and Beth fretted again. She remembered a variety show she'd seen on television once, a hypnotist who'd gathered a group of volunteers up on stage and made them do and say things that none of them could remember afterwards. It was funny, and mystifying, and Beth wondered if that would be Charlie's experience. If he'd wake up one morning after all this was over and remember nothing. Was that a good or bad thing? She didn't know.

Vela had called Charlie *special*, and he was right, but the word meant different things to different people. *Special* was another word for weird, or damaged, especially when referring to a child. *Slow*, was another word, one that a couple of doctors had used to describe Charlie's emotional development, and Beth couldn't help feeling that Vela was using Charlie, not only in the literal sense, but in the way a blind man would use a guide dog. Strangely, she also felt protective towards Vela. His physical size and recent vulnerability reminded Beth of a child, a defence mechanism perhaps, so she didn't have to think about the truth; that Vela was a being from somewhere else.

That thought had also caused Beth some anxiety. How far had he travelled? She had no idea how big the cosmos was, but if she picked the furthest star in the sky and stood on *that* rock, looking out into space, did it just carry on to infinity? It could drive a person mad thinking about it—

The knock at the door startled her. She put down her book and swung her legs off the bed. The man outside the door was smartly dressed in a suit, with a stiff collar and a narrow tie. He had tanned skin and wavy blonde hair that was neatly parted, and when he smiled his teeth were white and even. Beth thought she recognised him from the television, or maybe the films.

'Elizabeth Rolfe?' he said, smiling disarmingly.

'It's *Wakefield*,' she corrected him. 'I'm married,' she added, showing him her ring finger. She cringed. Why did she do that?

'I apologise, Missus Wakefield. Is Mister Wakefield here?' He looked over her shoulder into the room. Beth pulled the door closed behind her. The man's cologne could've stopped a charging rhino.

'What d'you want?'

'My employer would like to talk to you, about your uncle. A business matter. One that might be beneficial to you and your family.'

Jimmy Vaughn was warming his hands by the fire when Terry escorted the Rolfe woman to his table. Ten minutes earlier, Vic and Pat had cleared the snug with a combination of kind words and physical intimidation, and now they sat on a table just outside, barring entry to anyone else. Despite the semi-privacy, it was important that Vaughn was seen conducting his business in a public place, so he couldn't be accused of any heavy-handed tactics later on. This wasn't a pub back home. If it was, they'd be having a different conversation.

'Missus Rolfe?' Vaughn smiled, holding out his hand.

'It's Wakefield,' Terry corrected him.

'My apologies. Please, sit down.'

Vaughn could see the hesitation on her face, the suspicious eyes. She was wary, as most women were when their husbands weren't around. That was why he'd sent Terry up to her room, but only after the husband had pissed off out of the pub.

'What's this about, exactly?'

Vaughn smiled and pulled out a chair. 'Please, have a

pew.' The woman sat down. She wasn't bad looking, he decided. A bit thick around the thighs and bum, but a pretty face and nice blonde hair made up for it. Good pair of tits too.

'Your friend said something about a business matter?'

Vaughn took a seat opposite her. 'Can I get you a drink or something?'

She shook her head. 'My son is upstairs. I have to get back to him.'

'I understand. Nice kid too.' The woman didn't answer him, just stared back across the table. No lack of confidence there, he realised, and she was educated too, he could tell. Probably fancied herself as one of those independent types. He'd met a few in his time, women's libbers, mouthy slags most of them. A backhander around the chops usually put paid to that foolishness.

'It's about your uncle, Norman Rolfe.'

'Norman?'

'Tragic, what happened to him. My condolences.'

'Thank you.' She paused, then said, 'I hadn't seen him much, not since Charlie was born. We visited a few times, but that was about it. Norman was a lovely man, very kind. Generous too.'

'Very generous,' Vaughn echoed, thinking about Carol the croupier and the money that fat bastard had lavished on her. *His* money. Terry had taken her face off too.

'How did you know Norman?'

Vaughn smiled. 'He dropped dead in my casino. Luckily most of the punters had left for the evening.'

'Oh,' was all the woman said. The penny was dropping.

'Norman was a regular, see? Liked a punt or two. Used to travel up on the Friday, spend a couple of nights at the tables. Weekdays too. In fact, at the time of his death, he'd run up quite a bill.' He smiled at the woman, but it was an effort, because the more he thought about that disgusting tub of lard, the angrier he could feel himself getting.

'I'm sorry, Mister...?'

'Vaughn. Jimmy Vaughn.'

'I don't understand. Your friend said this was a business matter.'

'It is. The debt has to be paid, Missus Wakefield. I've had my people look into it, and they tell me you're the sole beneficiary of your uncle's estate, which means the debt is now yours to settle.'

She stared at him across the table, confusion clouding her eyes. *Come on, love, catch up.*

'I'm sorry, what is it you want from me?'

Vaughn gave her his best smile. 'Twenty thousand pounds.'

'Excuse me?'

He plucked a letter from the jacket hanging over the back of his chair. 'It's all there, all above board and legal.'

The woman took the letter and read it. It was on thick headed paper and drafted by Jimmy's solicitor. There was enough legalese in there to make any judge scratch his wig, but none of it would ever stand up in court. It would put the wind up a couple of country bumpkins, however.

'I don't expect it all at once,' Vaughn told her. 'We'll start with a lump sum, then after that we'll work out a payment plan.'

The woman passed the letter back across the table. 'This isn't our problem. Besides, there's no way we could afford that sort of money.'

Vaughn's smile slipped from his face. Patience had never been one of his strong points, especially when it came to money. He leaned across the table, his voice low. 'Well, you'd better come up with something fast, because I'm not leaving here until you've made it worth my while, got it?'

'I just don't—'

'Meeting's over,' Vaughn hissed, holding up his hand. Blondie got up and hurried from the table. He watched her disappear through the bar and up the stairs. Terry was staring at him.

'I thought you wanted to play it cool? Business-like?'

'Fuck all that,' Vaughn snarled. 'As soon as all them coppers leave this place, we'll go to work on them, proper.'

MAJESTIC TWELVE

Nash watched Phelan jogging through the heather towards him, dodging the soldiers who were busy laying a road of railway sleepers across the peak. By the time Phelan reached the crash site he was panting heavily.

'He's here,' the younger man puffed, nodding over his shoulder.

Nash turned towards the distant track and saw a figure heading out across the peak. Nash knew him by reputation alone, and on the few occasions he'd heard his name mentioned, it was spoken with a tone bordering on reverence. He turned back to Chambers and Phelan.

'This could be our chance to be part of something bigger, to work with the Yanks on a more permanent basis, so let's show them we can handle things. Syd, how are our communications looking?'

'Got a dedicated operator down at Oswestry exchange and Gladys is waiting by the phone in London. Anything we need, she'll make sure we get it. For everything else we can use the radio.'

'Good.'

'Also...' Phelan added, panting, 'representatives from Condor will arrive at RAF Machrihanish tomorrow. They want to see this for themselves.'

Nash nodded. He expected nothing less, but it wasn't often that the ultra-secret cabal gathered in numbers. Not publicly, in any case. Meetings normally took place behind the walls of stately homes and in the private confines of London's gentlemen's clubs. However, the phenomena of unidentified flying craft was extremely high on their agenda. Anyone who could unlock the secrets of that technology would wield significant global power. *Total power,* Nash corrected himself. If he could help deliver that for them, his place in future programs would be cemented.

The Yank was twenty yards away now. Nash muttered under his breath.

'Here we go, chaps.'

The American intelligence agent wore a wide-brimmed hat, and a belted raincoat buttoned to the neck. His trousers were tucked into wellington boots and he wore brown leather gloves on his hands. He put down the holdall he was carrying and held one out as Nash stepped forward to greet him.

'I'm Peter Nash, senior Condor field operative. This is my team, Ron Chambers and Syd Phelan.'

'Joe Fisk, Majestic Twelve,' the American said, smiling. Then he looked up at the craft a few yards away. 'Big sono-fabitch,' he muttered, as if he were looking at an everyday aircraft. 'Track's pretty narrow on the way up. You see any issues with clearance?'

'The transport team will jack up the craft on the back of the flat-bed,' Nash explained. 'That way it'll clear the stone walls all the way back to the village.'

Fisk looked across the moor, his eyes travelling around

the desolate landscape. 'We got lucky,' he said. 'Pretty barren up here. It ain't New Mexico though, so we need to work fast.'

'The temporary hard standing is almost complete,' Nash told him, pointing back to the fast-approaching track of railway sleepers. 'Another hour or two and we'll be able to bring the transport and winch vehicles across.'

'Get 'em to work faster,' Fisk ordered. He unzipped his holdall and yanked out a set of grey overalls. He took off his raincoat and pulled on the one-piece, buttoning it to the neck. Finally he snapped on a surgical mask and goggles. 'Show me the hatch,' he told Nash.

He led Fisk beneath the tarpaulins and shone his torch at the opening.

'Someone's been inside,' Fisk observed, waving his own torch at the muddy footprints around the hatch. 'Who was it?'

'A young farmhand,' Nash told him. 'He's being held at a local police station. He'll be transported to RAF Machrihanish when we leave.'

'Anyone else?' Fisk stared at Nash, the blue eyes above his mask cold and hard.

'Me,' Nash answered without hesitation. He knew that his reply could be a career breaker, that it could all end right here, but he couldn't stop himself. He'd built his career on trust and integrity, and win or lose, Fisk would know he was dealing with someone who had no problem telling the truth.

'A handful of locals got here before us,' he told the American. 'I saw the footprints and assumed one of them was still inside. I was concerned about vandalism, about the danger of an accidental power-up and potential catastrophic damage. I realise it's against protocol but I felt that preservation of the object was of the utmost importance.'

Nash waited, maintaining eye contact with Fisk, his career in the balance. After a moment or two Fisk nodded.

'It was the right decision,' the American told him. 'It'll go in my report, but your actions were warranted.' He braced his hands against the edge of the hatch. Just before he went inside he said to Nash, 'Did you see them? The entities?'

A relieved Nash nodded. 'I did.'

'Strange little guys, huh?' Then he smiled and ducked out of sight.

THEY CARRIED out the rest of their farming duties in relative silence. They filled up the feed troughs in the southern field, and Harry told Dougie to put a call into the vet as soon as the telephones were working again. The lambing season would be on them soon enough and the ewes needed a once-over to ensure they were okay. Dougie barely spoke a word, and Harry could feel the tension between them. It didn't bode well for the future.

They filled up the last of the troughs in the eastern meadow and climbed back into the tractor. Ten minutes later, Harry was turning into Dougie's courtyard and the tractor's engine rattled to a stop. The men jumped down and Harry headed towards the black Zephyr parked outside Dougie's farmhouse.

'Here, catch.'

Harry turned and caught the keys that Dougie tossed to him.

'What's this?'

'You take the car back to the village. I've got things to do around here.'

'You heard the police,' Harry warned. 'Essential works only, then it's back to *The Griffin*.'

'I'm staying,' Dougie told him as he marched towards the farmhouse. 'You do what you like.'

Harry knew it was pointless arguing. The man was bitter, and as stubborn as a mule. There was trouble ahead, that was for certain, but Harry had to put it all out of his mind. He had to get back to the village, find a way to get off the mountain and transport Vela to that portal of his. That's what mattered now.

Or was it? Was he *really* doing the right thing, jeopardising his family for the sake of a what? A being from another world? When he thought about it like that, it sounded crazy, stupid. Maybe he should just tell Nash, hand Vela over. Charlie would get over it eventually and maybe the country would benefit, learn something about the visitors. It was the patriotic thing to do.

He climbed into the Zephyr and started the engine. Who was he kidding? For some inexplicable reason, betraying Vela was the last thing he wanted to do. It was wrong, plain and simple. And it wasn't inexplicable either. No one falls eighteen thousand feet without a parachute and survives. Not without help.

He dropped the car into gear, turned out of the courtyard and headed down the track towards the village.

Dougie watched the car bounce down the hill until it was out of sight, then he dragged the curtain back across the window. He went to the drinks cabinet, grabbed a bottle and a glass, and poured himself a generous brandy. He flopped into his favourite chair, his boots dripping wet mud onto the threadbare rug. He looked around the small, dark parlour and realised that he had nothing to show for forty years of hard work. He lived in a rented house and worked a farm he had no financial stake in. His back was in bad shape and the arthritis in his fingers wasn't getting any better.

Nine months ago, Norman had brokered a deal to provide fresh meat and vegetables to the new-fangled supermarket shops in Wrexham and Chester. Norman's ex-wife and sons had emigrated to Australia years before, and he'd promised Dougie on more than one occasion that he would share in the spoils of the farm's improving fortunes.

And Dougie knew his boss liked a flutter, often waiting outside the bookies in Oswestry while Norman laid his bets, but the farm's growing prosperity had whetted his appetite for the big city gaming tables. Sometimes Norman would stay up in Liverpool for days. Sometimes he came back with a big smile on his face, but more often than not he would be in a slump. Whatever money he'd made off the back of his supermarket deals, Norman had pissed away gambling. No thought of Dougie, breaking his back to keep the farm profitable.

So when Norman had died, Dougie's hopes had soared. There had been no mention of a will, but Dougie assumed the farm would be his, and rightfully so. After all, who else was there? Then Harry Wakefield and his missus had turned up, dragging their spastic son with them, and that was that.

When the ship had crashed up on the peak, Dougie's hopes had spiked again, but he hadn't acted quickly enough. He'd been too preoccupied, his mind befuddled by what he'd witnessed, and by the time he realised the scale of the opportunity, the peak had been sealed off.

But not Harry Wakefield, Dougie recalled, swallowing the rest of his brandy. Harry had been first up there, and then he'd had the brass neck to tell Dougie to stay away. Why? It wasn't for Dougie's safety, nor the boys. No, it was because Harry had helped himself to something, the farm manager realised, and he didn't want anyone else cashing in. Something strapped to the front seat of his jeep. Maybe it was a dead Martian. Whatever it was, Harry must've stashed it, and Dougie thought he knew where.

He got to his feet and went outside. It was still sleeting, the cloud cover an ominous steel grey. He cut across the muddy courtyard and past the equipment sheds to the meadow beyond. He stood in the lee of a hay barn, his eyes roaming the sloping fields that stretched down towards the valley. Then he looked to his right, up across the meadow, towards the thin grey line of stone that marked the boundary of Harry Wakefield's property.

Dougie took one last look around, then set off across the meadow towards the distant farmhouse.

MEATHEADS

HARRY STEPPED inside *The Griffin* and saw Gavin Souter working a busy bar. He handed the car keys to him and went upstairs to his room. The door was locked. Beth let him in after he spoke through it.

'Everything okay?' he asked, as she bolted it behind him.

'Hello, Dad,' Charlie said, and went back to his drawing book. The radio was playing, a classical concert, and Beth turned the volume up as she took Harry's hand and led him towards the window. She stood close to her husband, keeping her voice low.

'There are some men staying in the pub. One of them came to the room, said he wanted to discuss a business proposition. He mentioned Norman's name.'

Harry said nothing, just let his wife talk. He could tell something was wrong.

'The men are from the casino in Liverpool, the one where Norman died. Apparently he ran up a debt, and now they want their money.'

'How much?'

'Twenty thousand.'

Harry's eyes widened. 'That's more than the farm's worth.'

'These aren't business people,' Beth warned. 'Moneyed, yes, but rough. Villains, I'd say. And the one in charge, this Vaughn man, he brought legal papers with him.'

'He's awake,' Charlie said.

Harry and Beth turned and looked at their son. The boy was stood by his bed, his drawing book abandoned, his brow creased with worry.

'He needs to go now, Dad. He says the air is killing him.'

Beth went to Charlie's side and held him close. 'What are we going to do, Harry? The police won't let us past the roadblocks, not until they've taken that thing off the peak. And I doubt Vaughn and his friends will leave Finnhagel empty-handed.'

Harry sat down on the bed and held them both. 'Get ready to leave. Dress warm, hats and coats, a couple of extra jumpers, gloves, scarves. Leave everything else here. I'm going downstairs, ask Meg to make us sandwiches for dinner, tell her we're eating in the room tonight. Then we'll sneak down the back stairs and leave.'

Beth shook her head. 'What about the roadblocks?'

Harry squeezed her hand. 'Trust me. We're getting out of here before it gets dark.'

Dougie stood in the wreckage of Harry's kitchen and cursed violently. He'd emptied every cupboard and drawer. He'd emptied the larder and the store cupboard. Broken crockery, tins of food, cutlery, pots and pans, vegetables, all of it was strewn across the tiles, but he'd found nothing. Dougie cursed again and booted a cabbage across the kitchen.

He took a moment to catch his breath and think. Harry must've taken a body from that spaceship—why else put it on the front seat? Then again, it could've been some Martian space gizmo, something that couldn't just be chucked in the back of the Land Rover. Because it was fragile, like that big china pot Norman had asked Dougie to pick up from the antiques shop in Oswestry last summer. The one that now lay in pieces in the hallway after Dougie had given it a vengeful kick. Delicate, like. But whatever it was, it wasn't down here.

He stamped upstairs into Harry's bedroom and started emptying the wardrobe, tossing clothes onto the bed, the floor, trampling it all beneath his muddy boots. He emptied boxes of photographs and mementoes, legal papers and knick-knacks. When the wardrobe was finally emptied, Dougie tipped it over onto the floor. Wood splintered, but there was nothing behind or underneath it. He did the same in the kid's room.

The spare room was empty, just a crumpled eiderdown on the bed, but he checked the wardrobe, just in case. He found suits and dresses, Harry's old RAF uniform in a bag. He dragged the wardrobe away from the wall and looked behind it. Nothing. Then his eye caught something under the bed. He bent down and picked it up, and it unravelled to the floor. A bandage. Dougie looked at the cotton wool pad, at the faint green stain. He sniffed it; it was a strange smell, slightly sweet. *Odd,* he thought. He dropped it on the floor and went back downstairs, searching each room once again, kicking his way through the debris, smashing glass and furniture as his frustration boiled.

Nothing.

He threw open the back door, his boots crunching across the broken glass of his forced entry. He spent another hour checking the outbuildings again, rooting amongst the piles of chopped logs, the feed and storage sheds, the equipment garage, but there was nothing hidden, no space gizmo, no little green body wrapped in dark material and stuffed out of sight.

Dougie took stock, scratching at the grey stubble of his chin as he stood in front of the house. He knew the farm like the back of one of his arthritic hands, far better than Harry bloody Wakefield, yet he'd come up empty. He'd practically dismantled the house too, which could mean only one thing; whatever Harry had stolen, he'd taken it with him down to *The Griffin*.

The more Dougie thought about it, the more he was convinced. When he'd driven Rita down to the pub, he'd noticed Harry's Land Rover parked tight against a corner wall of the car park. *Why?* There were lots of empty spaces, all of them much closer to the pub. Why park all the way over there?

Because he's hiding something in the back of it.

Something...

Dougie wrung his hands as he stood immobile in the falling rain. Something was nagging at him, something he'd seen but overlooked, something—

He bolted for the back door, bouncing off the walls as he charged upstairs and into the spare bedroom. He snatched the bandage off the floor and held it up again. Beth was a first-aider. That's how she'd met Harry, in that factory where they both worked. He'd fallen over or something, and she'd treated him. They'd told Dougie the whole boring story when they'd first arrived. Dougie stared at the soiled bandage in his hands. Beth had treated someone, right here in this room.

Not someone, Dougie realised. *Something!*

He dropped onto the bed, winded. Harry had found one of those things alive and brought it back here. *Jesus Christ, a real-life Martian,* Dougie gulped. That was worth a king's ransom, at the very least. Maybe even a million quid.

Now he had to make a choice. Option one—confront Harry, force him to cut Dougie in on any deal he might make. But things weren't so good between them, and when Harry discovered his house had been trashed, well, that would be that, and once again Dougie Booth would be out of pocket.

Which left option number two—tell the authorities. Not the local coppers, that would be a mistake. No, he needed to talk to that Nash bloke, show him that not all country folk were thick between their ears. That they could negotiate, thrash out a deal. It would also be the last roll of the dice. If this didn't work out, then the next ten years would be the same as the last, only much more painful. And Dougie didn't want that. He got to his feet, stuffed the bandage in his pocket and ran downstairs.

Outside, low cloud rolled down from the peak and swallowed Harry's farm. Dougie stood motionless outside the house, enveloped in silence as the damp grey mist swirled around him. He heard a faint clanking and grinding carried on the wind, coming from the distant peak. Dougie knew what that was. He also knew that Nash would be there right now.

He charged through the haze and out onto the track, heading uphill towards the army checkpoint at the edge of the forest.

MEG HANDED over a brown paper bag filled with ham, chicken and corned beef sandwiches, plus a few boiled eggs and some fruit. Harry weighed the bag in his hand.

'That's a bit more than I asked for,' Harry told her.

Meg smiled. 'Those government people are picking up the tab, so we might as well make the most of it, eh?'

'Might as well,' echoed Harry. 'We won't need anything else tonight, thanks Meg. We'll see you in the morning, okay?'

'Right you are,' Meg said, and disappeared back into the kitchen.

Harry headed back upstairs to the room. When he opened the door, the first thing he noticed were the lights. They were switched off. The second thing he saw were the silhouettes of two large men standing by the window.

'Beth—?'

'Relax, Mister Wakefield. No need to be alarmed.'

The gravelly voice belonged to the man sitting in one of the easy chairs. Beth was sat on the bed, her arms wrapped around Charlie. She looked small and frightened, as did his son. Harry snapped the light on and banished the gloom. The men by the window where heavies, that much was obvious, all thick necks and broken noses. There was another man to his right, a younger, blond man who smiled disarmingly.

'Who the hell are you?'

The man in the chair was looking at him, smiling. 'I think you know already. Or didn't your lovely wife fill you in?'

'It's Vaughn, right?'

'Bingo,' Vaughn said in the gloom. 'I wanted to meet you face-to-face, Mister Wakefield. Or can I call you Harry?' Harry said nothing and Vaughn continued. 'I'm not going to waste my breath repeating what I told your wife. Norman owes me a great deal of money. When he gambled in my casino he entered into a contract. All part of the membership small-print, you understand. Stops people taking liberties. Unfortunately for you, your uncle ran up a significant debt that requires settling. I'm here to get that process started.'

Harry shook his head. 'That's Norman's business. Nothing to do with us. I'm sorry, but I don't see how we can help you.'

Vaughn extracted a letter from his pocket and tapped it on his crossed leg. 'It's all legal and above board. I have every right to demand payment from the Rolfe estate. Now that you and your good wife are the legal owners, the onus is on you to repay Norman's debt.'

He held out the letter and Harry took it. He scanned it briefly, but he didn't understand much of the legalese. 'You'll have to give us some time. We need to read this, maybe talk to a solicitor.'

'You do what you like. In the meantime, I'm out of pocket. This little trip has cost me money, and with all the hullabaloo around here, it's cost me time too. And my time is precious, Harry. So the question is, how much are you going to give me as an upfront payment?'

Harry's heart raced. The blond man to his right was a big guy, not lumpy like the two meatheads at the window, but lithe, with sharp eyes. And then there was Vaughn himself, who radiated resentment. Beth was right, these men were gangsters, and Liverpool gangsters at that. They weren't to be messed with, that was for sure.

'I'm a farmer,' Harry explained, 'and I don't have much ready cash. I've probably got fifty quid up at the house, but you'll have to wait until these government people have left before I can get it. Everything is off-limits up there.'

Vaughn uncrossed his legs and got to his feet. He wasn't a tall man, but that didn't make him any less dangerous. Harry had met a lot of killers in his time, men who wouldn't hesitate to use a knife or a gun. War did that to some people, turned them into something else. Either way, Harry was convinced the man stood in front of him would have no trouble using violence to get what he wanted.

'Dad, we need to leave.'

Harry turned and looked at his son.

'It's okay,' Harry smiled, willing Charlie to be quiet. 'Let me deal with these gentlemen and then we'll talk, okay?'

'Vela's not well.'

Vaughn frowned. 'What's he blabbing on about?'

Harry tried to distract him. 'Listen, I understand that you're owed money, but this isn't the best time or place to discuss it. My son isn't well and it would be best—'

'I feel fine, Dad. It's Vela who's ill.'

'Vela?' Vaughn echoed. 'Funny name, that.'

'Sounds foreign,' the blond man said.

Harry took a step to his left and stood between Vaughn and Charlie. 'Let's get back to business, shall we?'

'Dad, we need to leave. Get to the portal.'

'Be quiet, Charlie,' Harry snapped.

Vaughn climbed out of his chair and took a step closer, his eyes drilling into Harry's. 'That's no way to talk to the kid. He's clearly upset about something, right kid?' He looked past Harry. 'What's the matter, lad? What's got you all worked up?'

Beth pulled Charlie tighter. 'Don't talk to him.'

'I'll go down to the bank in Oswestry as soon as the

roadblocks are lifted,' Harry promised. 'I can get you a couple of hundred pounds for your trouble. How does that sound?'

But his words were falling on deaf ears, Harry could see that. Vaughn's eyes had narrowed, and his nostrils twitched. He could smell something, and it stank of a lie. Harry felt the bag snatched from his hand. Vaughn unwrapped it and peered inside.

'Got enough food here for a couple of days,' he observed, dropping the bag on the bed. 'Thinking of doing a runner, lad?'

'Dad!' Charlie almost yelled. 'We have to go!'

Vaughn shouldered Harry out of the way and crouched down in front of Charlie. He smiled. 'What's the rush, little fella? Where are you off to, then?'

Charlie looked down at his booted feet. Vaughn reached into his pocket and yanked out a fistful of coins. He offered Charlie a shiny shilling. 'Here you go. That's for you. There's another one just like it if you tell me where you're going.'

'Leave him alone.'

Vaughn glared at Beth. 'Keep your mouth shut, sweet-cheeks.'

'Get away from my family,' Harry told him.

Vaughn straightened up, his hands balling into fists. 'You know something, soft lad, I'm getting a little tired of your bollocks. Now, you'd better tell me what's going on or my mate Terry here is going to go to work on your missus. And believe me, that's going to be very messy.'

'Jimmy.'

Vaughn ignored his blond friend and glared at Harry.

'Jimmy.'

Harry swallowed as Vaughn stepped closer. 'Well?' he growled.

'Jimmy.'

The gangster's head snapped around. 'For fuck's sake, *what*?'

'Look.'

Blondie was stood by Charlie's bed, holding up his drawing book. On the page was a coloured drawing of Vela, complete with large black eyes and three-fingered hands.

Vaughn stared at the drawing, his eyes narrowing, a cloud of confusion crossing his face. He looked at Charlie, then back to the drawing.

The penny dropped.

Jimmy Vaughn smiled.

NASH HEARD him grunting before he saw Fisk's hands appear at the edges of the hatch. A moment later the American crawled out of the ship and stood up. He dragged down his face mask and said, 'There's a missing entity.'

Nash frowned as Fisk shook himself out of his overalls. 'There's more than three of them?'

Fisk nodded. 'A similar craft came down in the desert in New Mexico several years ago. Same cockpit configuration inside, pretty much. Two guys in front and then two more slightly higher and offset. We've got three dead entities here but the fourth seat is empty. There's some organic residue down by the foot well, where the superstructure is crumpled. Looks like it sustained an injury. Chances are it's somewhere else in the craft but we won't know that until we open it up.'

'Any chance the thing is on the loose?' Chambers asked. 'Maybe it crawled out. Maybe it's hiding somewhere.'

'It would explain the open hatch,' Nash speculated.

Fisk shook his head. 'It's possible, but I doubt it. If one of them did get out, it won't last long, not in these conditions. We should sweep the mountain, to be sure.'

All three men ducked out from under the tarpaulin. The massive Antar was reversing slowly across the makeshift track towards the craft, shepherded by soldiers. The railway sleepers were slick with sleet and the ground was soft. The operation was a delicate one, Nash knew, and he'd feel a lot better once the craft was strapped to the back of the transport and they were off this bloody mountain. But the thought of an entity on the loose chilled his blood. They had to leave the area clean, otherwise Nash could find himself in Condor's bad books and side-lined for future operations.

The radio beneath the tarpaulin crackled. Chambers picked up the handset and keyed the transmit button.

'Go ahead, Syd.' Chambers listened for a moment, then said, 'Standby.' He turned to Nash. 'Frank's men are holding Douglas Booth down at the forest checkpoint. The loudmouth from *The Griffin*. Says he has information about the contents of the craft. Says it's a matter of urgency. He's asking to see you.'

Nash took the handset. 'Syd, it's me. Find out what he knows. If he's wasting time, have him arrested and shipped down to Oswestry.'

Nash waited, the handset held to his ear. He listened for several moments, then said, 'Bring him up.'

Fisk raised an eyebrow. 'Trouble?'

'A local farmer, one of the first up here. It was his farm-hand who went inside. Bit of a local bully, likes to run off at the mouth. Says he has information that he'll only talk to me about. My guess is, he wants to trade.'

Fisk's eyes narrowed. 'We can't risk some blabbermouth spilling his guts about this.'

'I'll deal with it,' Nash assured him.

They watched the Antar creeping across the moor towards them as soldiers used shovels to grit the railway sleepers and stop the tyres from slipping. It was a slow and delicate operation, but there was no other way of recovering the craft covertly. Nash willed the Antar to move faster. He turned away, and his eye roamed across the moorland and up to the peak. He imagined the entity crouched amongst the ferns somewhere up there, watching them. The hairs on the back of his neck stood on end.

Chambers pointed. 'Here comes Syd.'

Nash watched Phelan hurrying towards him. Striding next to him in a waterproof coat and flat cap was Douglas Booth. Nash stepped forward to meet them.

'Mister Booth has information,' Phelan told them.

'Important information,' Dougie added, red-faced and puffing. Fisk and Chambers stepped closer.

'Why don't you tell us what you know?' Nash began.

'Before we get to that, I want assurances that I'll be looked after. Money wise, that is.'

'We don't pay for information,' Nash told him. 'You have a duty as a British citizen to tell the authorities what you know, especially in this case. Our enemies are always watching, always listening, Mister Booth. The Soviets—'

'Spare me the Russian rubbish,' growled Dougie. He pointed to the craft that loomed above them. 'We all know that's a Martian ship you've got under there, so let's cut the nonsense shall we? I know something about the crew in there. About one of them in particular. Now, what's that worth to you blokes?'

Nash stared at the farm manager. Chambers and Phelan stared to. It was Fisk who broke the silence.

'Are you saying you have information regarding one of the occupants of this vehicle?'

Dougie's eyes lit up at the sound of Fisk's voice. 'A Yank! Now I know this is serious.' He jammed his hands in his pockets. 'I'm not saying another word until we make an arrangement.'

Nash knew he didn't have long. Every second counted and appealing to Booth's sense of patriotism was a waste of time. 'How much do you want?'

'A million pounds.'

Nash raised an eyebrow. 'For what?'

'For the whereabouts of your little green man. I know where he is, see?'

The Antar's engine growled as it reversed closer to the craft. Nash had to raise his voice as the others crowded closer. 'Where?'

'Money first,' Dougie insisted.

Nash turned to Chambers. 'Ron, get your notebook out and take down Mister Booth's particulars. I want the money transferred to his account by the close of business today.' He turned back to the farmer. 'You have my word as a senior official of her Majesty's government that you'll be paid for your information. Can we shake on it, Mister Booth?'

Dougie was already nodding, his eyes wide. 'You'll pay me today? A million quid?'

'We'll have to make two transfers of half-a-million each. That's the way government fund transfers work. Would you be agreeable to those terms?'

Dougie was hopping from foot to foot. 'Whatever you say, Mister Nash.'

'Good. So, where is this little green man?'

He pointed down the mountain. 'In the back of Harry Wakefield's Land Rover. At *The Griffin*.'

Nash's eyes narrowed. He stepped closer as the Antar rumbled towards them, belching diesel smoke and revving noisily. 'How can you be so sure?'

'Because I saw the thing sitting in Harry's front seat last night. Before you lot got here. He's been acting strange ever since. Then I found this in his house.'

Dougie pulled a bandage from his pocket and let it unravel to the ground. Fisk snatched it from him and inspected it. Then he looked at Nash and gave a very slight nod.

'It must have been wounded,' Dougie said. 'Harry's wife used to be a nurse. She probably patched him up.'

'*The Griffin*, you say?'

'He's there right now.'

Nash shook his head as the Antar's air brakes hissed. 'I can't hear you. Follow me.' He led Dougie up around the nose of the craft and down the other side. The others trailed behind. Nash stopped and turned, knee deep in snow and ferns.

'That's better,' he said, 'I can hear you now. So, you're sure about all this, Mister Booth? Everything you said is true? Because if it isn't, our deal is off.'

'You think I'd lie about something like this?' Dougie spluttered. 'No chance. Not with a million quid on the table.'

'I didn't think so.'

Nash pulled the Browning from his holster and shot him in the head. Dougie's knees buckled, and he folded into the ferns at Nash's feet, a sooty black hole just above his right eye. Nash holstered the gun and turned to Chambers.

'Ron, help me get him inside the craft, then cover the

hatch for transportation. Syd, get on the radio and get that pub sealed off right now. And have Wakefield and his family taken into custody. Let's go!'

Nash looked down at his feet. Dougie's mouth was open, his eyes wide with shock. It was the first time Nash had made a decision like this one, the first time he'd killed a civilian to keep a secret of this magnitude, and he wondered if it would be his last. He'd always been told that recovery, should it ever happen, was paramount, and the knowledge of that recovery of vital national security. Douglas Booth posed a threat to that, in Nash's assessment. Time would tell if he'd made the right decision.

He noticed someone standing next to him. Fisk was looking down at Booth's body.

'I'll take care of this. You need to go, get this situation contained. I'll supervise the loading, and then we'll rendezvous at the village. We all leave together, got it? That includes the entity.'

'Got it.'

Nash set off running across the peak.

'Who's that, lad?'

Vaughn held up the drawing book in front of Charlie. He tapped the strange crayon figure with a thick finger. 'Is that your friend?

Charlie stared at his boots. 'Yes.'

'Where is he, then?'

Harry's heart pounded. Vaughn was all smiles, his eyes focused on Charlie. He knew the gangster had already made his mind up that Vela was the real thing, and he could tell his son was on the verge of confirming it. If that happened, it was all over. Harry had a disturbing vision of the frail Vela being dragged out of the back of the Land Rover, of shrieking in pain, then being imprisoned somewhere, the rest of his life spent in misery, being prodded and poked like a lab rat. If he survived. Harry couldn't allow that to happen.

'Charlie, no more talking, okay?'

'You heard your Dad,' Beth added, squeezing Charlie's shoulders. 'Ask the nice man to give you your book back.'

Vaughn got to his feet. 'You'd better tell your boy to start

talking. Or do I have to persuade the kid some other way?'
He turned back to Charlie and leaned over him. 'Come on,
lad. Speak to your uncle Jimmy. You wouldn't want to see
your Mum and Dad get hurt now, would you?'

'Leave him alone,' Harry said, reaching for Vaughn's
arm.

'Hey!' The blond one, Terry, moved in fast and shoved
Harry back against the dresser. The mirror shook and Harry
steadied himself against the drawers. He held up his hands.
'Okay, okay! Take it easy,' he pleaded. 'Charlie, just tell the
nice man. Tell him what you know.'

'Harry!' Beth protested, but Vaughn was already grinning at the boy.

'You heard your Dad,' Vaughn said. 'Tell uncle Jimmy
all about your new friend.'

Terry moved in closer. The meatheads were transfixed.
Beth and Charlie were trapped in the eye of the storm. No
one saw Harry reach inside the drawer behind him.

'Come on, speak up,' Vaughn urged. 'What are you,
some sort of mute?'

Charlie looked up. Then he smiled. 'Look, Mum. Dad's
got a gun.'

Everyone spun around.

Harry pointed the Luger at Vaughn's chest. 'Beth, bring
Charlie over here now.'

One of the meatheads moved to block their path. Harry
extended his arm. 'Stand back, or I'll put a bullet in your
boss's chest.'

The meathead obeyed. Beth and Charlie got behind
Harry as he ushered them across the room. He reached into
his pocket and gave Beth the Rover key. 'Grab your coats
and the food and take Charlie downstairs,' he whispered in
her ear. 'Start the Rover, warm the engine. I'll be down in a

minute.' He waved the gun at the villains. 'All of you, in the corner. Move!'

The men sauntered towards the window and stood in a tight group, hands held low, eyes drilling into Harry. Vaughn was still smiling. 'You're making a big mistake, soft lad.'

Beth and Charlie pulled their coats and hats on and headed for the door. Vaughn's eyes flicked between Harry, the gun, and Charlie. The meatheads tensed like athletes, ready to explode across the room. Harry knew he wouldn't be able to stop them all if they charged.

Then it would be over.

Nash rattled the phone cradle in Harry's house. The wreckage had been a surprise, and he suspected that someone, probably Booth, had searched in vain for the entity. He jiggled the cradle again. No one at the exchange in Oswestry was picking up.

'Damn it!' He turned to Chambers. 'Ron, go with Hughes down to the pub. I want Wakefield and his family in custody immediately, and I want that car park cordoned off.'

Chambers left the house on the run. Engines roared and lights blazed out on the track as Chambers piled into a jeep and headed down the mountainside at speed, a truck full of soldiers following close behind.

Phelan stood on the porch, the military radio at his feet.

'Syd, radio those idiots in Oswestry. See if they can contact any of their uniforms in the village. If they can, get them to surround the pub. No one goes in or out. Use any means necessary.'

· · ·

'THINK ABOUT WHAT YOU'RE DOING,' Vaughn snarled. 'Right now you're looking at a couple of broken legs. If you're smart, it'll end there. If you're not, then the damage extends to your wife and kid. Trust me, soft lad, you don't want me as an enemy.'

Harry ignored him, rattled the gun at Blondie. 'You, tie your friends up.'

'How am I supposed to do that?'

'Tear up some bloody sheets!' Harry snapped.

Blondie tutted. 'That's vandalism. I can't do that.'

Vaughn pointed at Harry's gun. 'That's a Kraut piece, right? A Luger.'

Harry nodded. 'And I know how to use it, so don't test me.'

No one moved. Blondie wasn't lifting a finger to tie up his friends. One of the meatheads had moved a little closer too. The fact was, the gun intimidated none of them, and that frightened Harry more than anything.

Beth and Charlie would be in the Rover by now, and the light outside was fading fast. He needed to buy them a couple more minutes, just to be sure. Then he would make his move. When he did, Vaughn would be right on his tail. Harry knew it would be close, and the odds were stacked in the villains' favour.

'You're thinking how you're going to get out of this,' Vaughn told him, a smile plastered across his pockmarked face. 'Well, you're not, but a couple of broken legs is a small price to pay for crossing me. Ask anyone in Liverpool. You're getting off light.'

'Shut your mouth,' Harry ordered, edging back towards the door.

'Tell me where that Martian is and I'll write off your uncle's debt. I can't say fairer than that.'

Harry reached behind him, his fingers scrabbling for the door handle. The meatheads advanced slowly, their bodies tense, chins lowered, like a pair of rhinos about to charge. Harry's gun hand stiffened.

'Not another step,' he warned.

Vaughn shook his head. 'Don't think about running, lad. You won't make it. Neither will your wife and kid.'

Harry twisted the handle.

Vaughn said, 'He doesn't have the bottle, lads. A tenner to the one who brings him down.'

The meatheads roared and charged. Harry fired twice, each bullet finding a meaty thigh. Blondie came around the outside, leaping over the beds. Harry switched aim and fired again, the gunshots deafening in the small room, the bullet tearing a chunk out of the wall. Blondie slipped and fell between the beds. Vaughn had already ducked out of sight. The meatheads were rolling on the carpet, yelling in furious agony—

Harry flung open the door and ran for the stairs. He charged down them and into the hallway at the back of the pub. Outside, he pushed over a stack of empty beer barrels and they bounced and rolled across the cobbled courtyard.

Lights blazed in the car park. Harry sprinted, gun in hand. He heard shouting behind him and police whistles shrilled on the darkening sky. He wrenched open the door of the Rover and climbed in.

'Where's Charlie?' Harry yelled.

'He's in the back. Just go!'

Harry jammed the Rover into gear and stamped his foot on the accelerator, just as Vaughn and Blondie stumbled out of the back door. Their hands clawed the air as the Rover shot past them and down the alleyway towards the village high street. Harry yanked the wheel to the left, back wheels spinning wildly on the wet street.

'Where're you going?' Beth shouted as she hung on.

'Trust me!' Harry told her, his eyes never leaving the road. Up ahead, the police roadblock loomed, two cars parked at angles across the street. Beyond them lay the track and home. Harry saw lights blazing down the hillside towards the village, saw the army truck swaying as it followed a jeep at speed. He caught movement to his right—policemen on foot, truncheons drawn, running towards him. He couldn't go straight, couldn't turn around, couldn't head back down the hill, but that was fine with Harry. He knew exactly where he was going.

Soldiers were streaming past the roadblock. Harry sped towards them, pulling the wheel hard left as they scattered. Beth screamed as the Rover mounted the pavement and shot down a narrow alleyway between two shops. Harry gritted his teeth as the vehicle bounced off the rough stone walls and then they were clear again, scattering chickens across a yard before crashing through a fence and into a muddy field.

Harry's hands slapped at the wheel, desperately trying to bring the Rover under control as the back end swung wildly and threatened to roll them over. Harry gritted his teeth—if he'd learned anything these past few months, it was how to drive a vehicle over soft sloping ground.

He tamed the Rover's wild rush downhill with some smart footwork and fast hands, gearing down to gain traction. The engine roared. The tyres bit. Beside him, Beth was cursing and praying all at once.

'You okay back there, Charlie?'

Behind the hessian curtain, Charlie said, 'Yes, Dad, but you have to go faster.'

'Tell me where to go, Son. Tell me where the portal is.'

'Anglesey.'

Harry and Beth shared a look. 'That's a hundred miles away.'

'Eighty. Drive fast, Dad,' Charlie told him.

Harry gripped the wheel as the Land Rover bounced down the hill. Through the sweep of beating wipers he saw the black, boiling ribbon ahead. Beth's voice went up a fearful notch.

'Harry, the river!'

'I know,' Harry told her. 'Everyone, hold on!'

Beth gripped the dashboard. The Rover dipped and nosed into the fast-moving body of water at speed, and then they were bouncing and rolling across the shallow rocky bed until the wheels hit the soft ground on the opposite bank.

Then it stopped dead.

The engine whined and roared, wrapping the vehicle in a fog of steam.

'Come on!' Harry yelled, his foot jammed on the accelerator. He glanced in his mirror, saw torch beams waving across the field behind him. He imagined police cars screaming down the mountain, desperately trying to cut them off.

'Please,' Harry whispered, and then the tyres bit and the vehicle lurched up the shallow slope, its headlights picking out a muddy track in the darkness. Harry gunned the engine, and they were level again, bumping and swerving between the trees. After a couple of hundred yards the track widened, and then a gravel lay-by opened up ahead of them. Beyond that, traffic moved in both directions along the Oswestry Road.

Harry eased the Land Rover out onto the tarmac and merged with the early evening traffic. It was light and moderately paced, and Harry kept to the speed limit. Slowly his heart rate began to settle a little.

'Everyone okay?'

Beth looked at him, her face barely lit by the dashboard lights, by the traffic passing in the opposite direction. 'Bloody good job, Harry Wakefield.'

'Thought we might need an escape route, just in case, but we're not out of the woods yet. We need to get through town and out the other side before we head west.'

'We have to make a stop,' Beth told him, 'at the infirmary in Oswestry. Vela needs help.'

Harry winced. 'In the centre of town? It'll be crawling with police. Besides, the place'll be closed by now.'

Beth reached across and squeezed Harry's knee.

'That's why we're going to break in.'

By THE TIME Nash got to Finnhagel, the fish had already slipped the net.

He stood by the wreckage of the smashed gate and looked down the hill where muddy tyre tracks weaved a reckless path into the darkness. He saw torch beams bouncing here and there as police officers pursued Wakefield's jeep on foot. A ridiculous exercise, he knew. He turned to the senior officer next to him.

'What are his options?'

The policeman pointed into the darkness. 'South will take him towards Welshpool, east to Shrewsbury, north to Wrexham. I've ordered rolling road blocks for fifty miles. The vehicle registration number has been circulated and off-duty officers have been called in. We'll get him.'

'What about west?'

The Chief Constable shrugged in the darkness. 'Not

much between here and the coast, except the port at Holyhead. I've alerted local police and customs.' There was a pause, then the senior policeman said, 'How d'you want to handle the two casualties?'

'Send them to the hospital.'

'The other two, Vaughn and O'Gorman, they're known villains.'

'Not my concern,' Nash told him. He watched the distant torches sweeping across the hillside below. 'Call your men back, Chief Constable. Redeploy them locally, on every road in the area. Search every farm, every cottage, every track. I need that vehicle found and found quickly.'

Nash headed back up the alleyway towards the high street. The windows overlooking the centre of Finnhagel were dotted with curious faces. There was a small crowd outside *The Griffin* that was ringed by police officers. Nash doubted that this community had ever experienced such excitement, and excitement made tongues wag. It was the last thing Nash needed. What was required was a return to normality, and quickly.

Chambers and Phelan fell in beside him as Nash marched towards Hughes and his soldiers. Nash motioned for the officer to join him a short distance away.

'What's the story, Frank?'

'I've got half my unit down here. The rest of them are up on the peak, waiting to escort the craft. How do you want to play this? I could reassign some men to help hunt this Wakefield chap down.'

'I'll need you and a couple of your best men, for security. Sidearms only, and bring a radio. Send the rest of them on to Scotland with the craft. Fisk will be in charge.'

'Understood.'

As Hughes marched away, Nash turned to Phelan.

'Syd, I want you set up at the police station in Oswestry. Have Gladys standing by the phone in London and get a radio from Hughes. Put a call in to Condor liaison and explain the situation. Let them know that we'll all be at RAF Machrihanish sometime tomorrow.'

'That's not a lot of time,' Chambers warned. 'Wakefield's probably miles away by now. If he goes to ground it could take weeks, maybe months to find him.'

Nash nodded. 'Nevertheless, our benefactors will expect us to capture this entity. They'll want to see it, and the craft, for themselves. We can't put them off, or give them excuses. Wakefield's travelling in a ten-year-old, slow-moving Land Rover with his wife and son, and the roads will soon be flooded with police cars. We'll find them in the next twelve hours.'

Nash thrust his hands in his pockets and looked along the village high street. The sleet fell steadily now, and he noticed flakes of snow spiralling to the ground. If they were lucky, they would beat the weather.

If they were luckier, the weather would beat Harry Wakefield.

FISK LEANED in close to the Antar driver and shouted above the roar of the diesel engines. 'What's your name?'

'Corporal Stone, sir.'

'You happy with the winching set up, Stone? With this goddamn weather closing in, we might only get one shot at this.'

Stone was standing on the back of his trailer, operating the winching equipment mounted at the rear. He was wrapped up in a military parka, hood up, his nose and mouth covered with a green scarf. He slapped the metal flanks of the winch with a gloved hand. 'I can drag a sixty-ton battle tank up on here with this thing.' He jerked a thumb over his shoulder. 'If we can't manage it, we'll call up the winch truck and use both. Either way, we'll get her moving, sir, don't you worry.'

Fisk slapped Stone on the arm. 'I'm paid to worry. Let's do this.'

He jumped down from the trailer. Whistles blew and soldiers backed away from the craft. Snow gusted through a cone of light mounted on the back of the Antar's cab. Fisk scrambled further up the hill so he was looking down on the operation. The buried nose of the craft had been dug out and now lay crumpled and exposed to the elements. The rest of the ship was swathed in sheets of tarpaulin, all held in place by ropes and thick transportation straps. The craft itself was barely visible. Fisk put his fingers in his mouth and whistled, spinning another finger in the air.

Diesel smoke belched as the winch motor roared. Straps and chains sprung taut as the winch jib raised up into the air. Fisk saw the crumpled nose of the craft shudder, and then it was moving, twisting around to face the back of the trailer. Mud and vegetation fell away as the craft lifted slowly off the ground. A whistle blew, and the winch engine died. The craft dangled just above the ground, twisting in the wind. Fisk ran back down to the trailer and shouted up at Stone.

'What the hell's the matter?'

Stone leaned over, his hands gripping the winch levers. He shook his head. 'Standard procedure,' he told Fisk, his words whipped away by the wind. 'Gives us a chance to test the weight, make sure the rig is stable.'

'So, are we good?'

Stone grinned and pointed to the craft. 'She's as light as

a feather. Like she's filled with helium. Strangest thing I've ever seen. We should be loaded up and mobile in less than half an hour.'

Fisk gave the man a thumbs-up and scrambled back up the slope. This time he kept moving, up towards the peak itself, stopping a few yards short of the edge. The wind plucked at his coat, at his hat.

The Berwyn Mountains stretched away into the distance, inky black mounds set against a dark sky. Below his feet, the ground fell away steeply and sharply towards the invisible valley below. There wasn't a single light to be seen, not a single road or dwelling. They'd been lucky, Fisk knew. Three *fallen angels* in fifteen years and all of them in remote, barely accessible areas. It was a sign, he believed. Mankind just wasn't ready for such a revelation. If the existence of such crafts and beings were made public, it might destabilise everything; countries, governments, economies, belief systems, and that wouldn't do anyone any good. Best to keep it under wraps until such time that the world was ready. Fisk doubted that would be anytime soon.

A couple of hundred yards below him, engines growled and chains clanked, and he saw the tarp-draped craft settle onto the back of the trailer. Dark figures swarmed around it, Lilliputians tying down the giant in their midst. Powerless, if it ever woke up.

The wind gusted across the peak, and snow swirled on the cold air. Fisk pulled his collar a little tighter and headed back down to the crash site.

GAS AND AIR

'Are you sure about this?'

'Just give me something to break the window.'

Harry had parked in the black shadows of an abandoned mill. Across a stretch of weed-choked ground was the delivery entrance of the Oswestry Infirmary. He opened the back door of the Rover and grabbed a metal tyre iron.

'Here. Wrap your scarf around it before you use it, deaden the noise a little. And make sure you wear your gloves.' He couldn't help himself and asked again. 'Are you sure you want to do this, Beth?'

'I know what I'm looking for. Besides, it's the only way he'll survive.'

Harry took a deep breath. 'Okay. Go. And be quick.'

He watched Beth jog across the waste ground and disappear down an alleyway alongside the infirmary. Beth was right, Harry tagging along would be pointless, and dangerous for Charlie and Vela. As Harry waited, he began tugging clumps of grass and bits of branch from the grill and wheel arches. The sleet was doing its best to wash the rest of the mud off, although that didn't matter much around here. Mud-splattered land Rovers were ten-a-penny. He didn't touch the filthy registration plates.

He climbed into the back of the Rover and sat next to Charlie. The engine was still running, and the heater pumped warm air inside the vehicle. His son had made an opening in the pile of hessian and he saw the pale disc of Vela's face. His eyelids fluttered and his tiny nostrils inflated and deflated like bellows. Harry couldn't tell if his eyes were focused or not. He put his hand on his son's neck and gave him a reassuring squeeze. 'He's going to be okay, Charlie. Mummy will help him get better.'

'Vela thanks you,' Charlie told him.

'Tell him I'm returning the favour.'

Charlie's chubby face beamed. 'He can hear you, Dad.' Then he frowned and said, 'What do you mean, *favour?*'

'I'll tell you later. Vela knows, I think.'

White light filled the back of the Land Rover and Harry's heart leapt. The light flared and faded, and Harry saw police car out on the nearby road, heading towards the centre of Oswestry. Then he saw something else. It was Beth, hurrying across the wasteland with a cylinder in her arms. Harry climbed out of the back and ran to meet her. That's when he heard the clanging of a burglar alarm.

'Quickly!' she puffed, handing Harry the cylinder.

He laid it in the back of the Rover and helped Beth inside. He got back behind the wheel and kept the lights off as he drove across the mill's waste ground, only flicking them on when they bumped back onto the main road. He headed away from town, avoiding the main routes and keeping to the side streets.

He worked his way west until he found the B4579, a

narrow, unlit tarmac capillary that would take them across the border and into Wales. Sleet was still falling through the headlights, and Harry knew that the road ahead would be treacherous, but time was of the essence. Unless Beth could work her magic. Behind him he could hear the rasp of tape and the snip of scissors, her quiet words to Charlie, the metallic clanking of the rolling cylinder on the floor of the vehicle.

'How're we doing back there?'

'Just keep your eyes on the road,' Beth told him from behind the curtain.

Harry obeyed, searching the route ahead, noting the signs, the road markings, his speed, the time. All he could do now was drive, and pray things worked out.

The lights and houses of Oswestry thinned out, and soon there was nothing to be seen on either side of the empty road. The Land Rover kept heading west, dwarfed by dark, unseen hills that climbed up towards the Welsh border.

Nash watched the Antar nose down the hill and rumble into Finnhagel, its flashing yellow grill lights washing across the stone facades of the village high street and competing with the pulsing blues of the police vehicles. Fisk was riding shotgun in the lead jeep and Nash stepped into the road and waved him down. Fisk climbed out, and both men stood with their hands in their pockets as the Antar rumbled past, the craft lashed to its trailer completely shrouded in tarpaulins, its shape cleverly disguised by strategically placed crates and poles.

'Everything okay?' Nash asked.

'It went like clockwork,' Fisk told him. 'You got a good team.'

'They've been drilled extensively.'

'What's the situation on our missing person?'

Nash filled him in on everything, including Wakefield's violent getaway. Fisk nodded and said, 'Excuse the cliché but *dead or alive* are your only two choices right now, so don't let me keep you. Good luck.'

Fisk climbed back into the jeep and it jerked away from the kerb, heading downhill after the convoy. The grumble of engines and flashing lights slowly faded, and peace returned to the village once more. Tomorrow, police officers would hand out leaflets thanking the villagers for their cooperation, urging them to be vigilant for suspicious persons or vehicles and reinforcing the Cold War narrative. A substantial donation would also be made to the Parish council, and local luminaries would be invited to London on an all-expenses paid trip to meet 'government officials', after which they, and their spouses, would spend the rest of the weekend in a swanky West End hotel. Silences would be bought, and lips would remain firmly sealed. And if the carrot didn't work, there was always the stick.

Nash climbed into the waiting Zephyr. Chambers got behind the wheel and started the engine, flicking the heater on to full blast.

'How will we play the Booth business?' the security man asked.

'Nervous breakdown, radiation poisoning, perhaps. Maybe we'll link him to a Russian spy ring, but that's for others to decide. What matters now is finding our little grey friend.'

Chambers glanced at his boss. 'It's funny, but until last night I'd always assumed they'd be green.'

Nash smiled in the dark as the car wound its way down the mountain.

'Now we know better.'

THE VESSEL EXITED the mouth of the intra-galaxy wormhole fourteen thousand miles from the dark side of the moon and slowed its forward velocity to sixty-eight thousand miles per hour. It had travelled twenty-eight light years to reach the edge of Earth's gravitational influence and had done so in a relatively short space of time. After all, both planets were located in the Milky Way, so they were practically neighbours.

The vessel was huge by Earth standards, and shaped like a giant wedge of slate, its black surface rippled with channels and indentations, visible scars from its countless journeys through dead star-fields and the dying rage of exploding suns. It had visited this solar system many times across the millennia, and its occupants had taken a specific interest in the species that inhabited the third planet from this particular sun. So, when the distress call had beamed across the galaxy, a rescue mission had been quickly organised. This was not an unusual occurrence for the galactic explorers who inhabited the exoplanet in the *Gliese* constellation, a planet that was five times the size of Earth and technologically advanced by more than ten thousand years. Sometimes the distress calls came from much further away, and sometimes the advance parties could not be saved, but that hasn't been the case with Earth, not until recently.

The vessel slowed, drifting past Earth's moon at fifty thousand miles an hour, harnessing the planet's gravitational pull to draw it ever closer. Inside the vessel, entities prepared to launch a much smaller vessel, similar to the one that had been lost. A crew would board it, and when the time was right, they would pilot it silent and unseen down to the Earth's surface.

All they needed was the location of the gateway.

SNOWDONIA

'*RESPIRATORY FUNCTION HAS BEEN RESTORED.*'

The voice in his head startled Harry, and he almost swerved off the road. Instinctively, his fingers touched his nose and ears, checking for blood. They were clear, and Harry had to remind himself that Vela meant them no harm. At least, he hoped that was still the case.

'Beth, talk to me, love.'

'Pull over,' she ordered him from behind the curtain. 'I'm going to sit up front.'

He looked ahead through the beating wipers. They were over the Welsh border now, and the world outside the Land Rover was black and impenetrable. The wet tarmac wound its way through the wild, invisible countryside, then Harry saw a cutting ahead by the side of the road. He pumped the brakes and eased the Rover carefully onto the muddy verge.

Harry left the engine running and jumped out. A cold wind gusted over the black hills around him. He opened the back door and Beth swung her legs out and hurried into the passenger seat. He glimpsed Charlie wrapped up in the hessian next to Vela.

'Are you all right, Son?'

Charlie gave him a thumbs up. 'Yes, Dad.'

Harry smiled despite himself. He closed the door and stepped out into the wet road. He heard a noise, a rushing sound, and then the sky lit up—

The car swept around a nearby bend. Harry climbed in behind the wheel just as the vehicle flashed past. A dark car. With lettering on the door.

'Police,' Harry cursed, jamming the gear-lever into first and spinning the wheels back onto the tarmac.

'Go!' Beth urged, checking her mirror.

Harry glanced at his own and thought he saw the flare of red brake lights but he couldn't be sure. The road ahead twisted sharply downhill. No wonder he didn't see or hear the car coming. He drove quickly but carefully, using the whole width of the road, his headlights on full beam. When the road straightened, he put his foot down and checked his mirrors. All he saw was darkness. He began to breathe a little easier.

'How's Vela?'

'Stable. I've got him on oxygen. Did you hear him in your head?' Harry nodded. 'Me too. It's such an odd feeling.'

'What about Charlie?'

'He's fine. He seems completely unfazed by everything, even that unpleasantness with Norman's friends.' Beth turned and looked at Harry. 'I never knew you had a gun.'

'I never told you. Truth is, I'd pretty much forgotten all about it until we moved to Finnhagel.' He saw a bend in the road ahead, and he geared down for the turn. 'It's a souvenir from the war. After Jerry abandoned our POW camp, I was one of the first to explore the admin buildings. They'd left in a hurry and I found the gun in a guard room locker. I took it, just in case, and kept it ever since.'

Beth turned away and stared out at the darkness. 'Did you kill someone? Back there, I mean. In *The Griffin*. I heard shots.'

Harry shook his head. 'I winged a couple of 'em, that's all. I had no choice.'

'*Winged?* This isn't the films, Harry. If one of those men dies, they could hang you for it.'

'They rushed me, for God's sake. It was them or us.'

'Keep your voice down.'

Beth reached out and put her hand on the back of his neck. She stroked it affectionately, her fingers warm on his skin. Then she pulled her hand away, her eyes drifting back to the darkness outside. 'Either way, we're in a lot of trouble. Shootings, burglary, running from the police; we could both go to prison. That's unthinkable. I won't be separated from Charlie. Not ever.' She chewed a nail as she stared into the void. 'Yet I can't help feeling that what we're doing is right. That it's worth the risk.'

'I feel the same.'

'And then I think about afterwards, when all this is over. Those men from the Air Ministry, they seemed pretty hostile. I imagine they'll be furious knowing what we've done. And that Vaughn creature will still want his money. What are we going to do?'

Harry reached out and squeezed Beth's hand. 'We'll worry about that later. Right now, we need to get our friend to this portal thingy, whatever that is.'

'He told you already,' Charlie tutted behind the curtain. 'It's an off-world gateway. Vela says you need to focus your mind, Dad.'

Harry and Beth exchanged a look. She pulled back the curtain. 'Did you hear me and your Dad talking, Charlie?'

'No. Vela was speaking in my head, telling me about his planet. It sounds brilliant. Can we go, Mum? He says we can.'

Harry felt a chill prickle his skin. *Can we go?* Such an innocent thing to ask, to which there was literally no answer. *Could* we go? he asked himself. The Russians and Americans had both put men into orbit around the earth, but the effort was huge and costly, and required years of training, not to mention the physical and mental preparation. Charlie was making it sound like a trip to the seaside. Then again, for Vela and his people, maybe it was just like that.

'We'll see,' Harry told his son. He saw Beth looking at him, wide-eyed, and he shrugged. 'We'll have to go during the school holidays,' he told her, and she smiled. He had to make a joke of it because the reality was too much to think about.

After a moment, like Oz behind his curtain, Charlie spoke again.

'Vela says there's a car following us. He says there's a road ahead, on the right. It looks like a track but we can use it as a shortcut.'

'Must be that police car,' Harry muttered to Beth.

She shook her head. 'How can Vela possibly know?'

'No idea, but I'm going to take his word for it.'

Harry leaned over the wheel and peered through the windshield. The wipers were working hard and sleet gathered in an icy crust around the edges of the glass. It was like driving through a tunnel, the stone walls either side of the road getting ever closer. He checked his mirrors. Nothing.

'Are you sure someone's behind us?'

'Yes. Slow down,' Charlie told him.

Harry took his foot off the accelerator, and then he saw it, a gap in the stone wall ahead. He braked hard and turned onto the track.

'Turn your lights off. Keep driving, slowly. And don't touch the brakes.'

Harry did as he was told, confused and anxious about the role his son was playing, one that was far too adult for his young and sensitive mind. But was Charlie *really* being manipulated? Or was Vela protecting Harry and Beth from having their brains turned to mush by his telepathy? Harry put it out of his mind. He had to trust in Vela. After all, he needed the Wakefield's more than they needed him.

The world outside turned black as the Land Rover crawled along a well-used rural pathway. Sleet had settled as snow on the grass divide between the tyre tracks, and the pale white line meant Harry could steer the Rover safely enough if he kept his speed down and eyes on the track.

'There they are,' Beth said, and then the countryside lit up behind them as a car passed along the main road at speed, its siren wailing, its blue light pulsing in the dark. Then the light faded, and the car was swallowed by the night.

Harry blinked a couple of times and waited for his vision to settle. When it did, the track revealed itself once again as it wound its way into the darkness. 'Is Vela sure about this?'

'One hundred percent,' Charlie told him. 'Follow this track until you reach another main road. Head for Bangor, Dad. Vela will show us the way from there.'

'If you say so, Son.'

'We do.'

Harry kept the snow-crusted grass centred between his

wheels. The landscape outside was no longer black. On either side, beyond the stone walls, snowy fields rose all around him. They were heading uphill, and Harry hoped that the going wouldn't get too treacherous.

'How about one of those sandwiches then?'

Beth reached behind the curtain and retrieved the paper bag. She handed out corned beef and chicken sandwiches to Charlie and Harry, and everyone was suddenly reminded of how hungry they were.

'What happens? After the portal thingy?'

'I don't know,' Harry said between mouthfuls. 'We hand ourselves in, I suppose.'

'We need to take precautions, protect ourselves. If we're going to Bangor, we could find a reporter. Tell the whole country what happened.'

Harry shook his head. 'I can't do that, Beth. That Nash bloke was right; whatever happens this is a national security issue. If we make this public, we could be helping the Soviets, and then we'd be in very serious trouble.'

Beth's sandwich froze halfway to her mouth. 'The Russians now? God, I just want everything to go back to the way it was.'

'I'm not sure it will,' Harry told her. 'And even if it does, we'll be looking for a new manager. I'm done with Dougie. He pretty much told me he resents us being here.'

Beth swallowed a mouthful of food. 'Why?'

'He thinks Norman owes him, for all the years of work he's put in at the farm. He thought he might get something in the will. At least that's the impression I got.'

'That will was a surprise for all of us.'

'Who knew your uncle was a big-time gambler?'

Beth grimaced. 'Not us, that's for certain.'

'We could always scale down, sell everything we can't manage, pay off that Vaughn bloke.'

'If we lose the supermarket contract, we'll struggle.'

'Maybe we can renegotiate?'

Beth took a deep breath and sighed. 'I can't think about any of that right now. I'm tired and cold and I just want this to be over.' She turned and pulled back the curtain. Charlie was buried beneath the hessian alongside Vela, both of them keeping warm. 'Are you okay in there, Charlie Wakefield?'

'Yes, Mum. Vela says he feels a lot better. He says you will too.'

'I hope he's right,' Beth said, and dropped the curtain back into place.

Harry looked at his wife and winked. 'I think someone's going to miss our friend when he goes,' he whispered.

Beth frowned. 'Something else to deal with.'

Harry gripped the wheel a little tighter as he felt the Land Rover crest a hill and drop over the other side. The ground fell away before them, a patchwork of snowy white squares, fields and walls, but no lights, no houses. The scene reminded Harry of another night, many years ago, when the plane had burned, and he'd leapt out into the freezing night air. He remembered the ground below, rushing up to meet him, a landscape so similar to the one that now stretched ahead of them.

And he remembered what he saw, before he lost consciousness at eighteen thousand feet.

The silent black craft that hurtled towards him.

HUNTING PARTY

THE FORD ZEPHYR was travelling west at sixty miles an hour through a curtain of sleet that threatened to turn to snow at any moment.

Chambers was behind the wheel, his eyes fixed on the road, on the police car ahead, its blue light sweeping the darkness. Behind the Zephyr, Hughes and his soldiers followed in a military jeep. The convoy was headed west on the A5 towards the Menai Strait and the sparsely populated island of Anglesey. The traffic was light, the weather deterring all but determined and duty-bound travellers from venturing out onto the roads.

Nash watched the dark countryside passing outside his window. *Where are you?* he wondered. *Are you cold, tired, frightened, desperate?* All of the above, perhaps. Nash had never tried to second-guess a being from another world before, but the involvement of Harry Wakefield and his family made that process a little more predictable, dictated as they were by earthly constraints. But Harry Wakefield was no ordinary citizen, Nash had discovered.

Gladys had pulled Wakefield's MoD records and

Phelan had filled Nash in over the radio. That's when the penny had finally dropped. His meeting with Wakefield had rung a distant note of familiarity, one that now made sense.

The RAF top-gunner who'd fell to Earth during the war.

Eighteen thousand feet without a parachute, his fall broken by trees and a deep snowdrift, his injuries amounting to not much more than a bruised knee and some scratches. He'd been captured, and for a while he'd become a minor celebrity amongst his captors and fellow prisoners, but he'd spent the rest of the war in an Allied POW camp before being liberated in forty-five. Wakefield had made a couple of radio appearances after the war, but as a fellow RAF officer, Nash remembered the legend of his fall. It was one of many strange and bizarre brushes with Fate and death that soldiers, sailors and airmen had experienced throughout the six years of global conflict.

But Wakefield wasn't the only survivor from that doomed Lancaster.

The navigator, Philip Spencer, had also survived, parachuting safely to earth and ending up behind the wire of another POW camp a hundred miles from Wakefield's. Over the radio, Phelan had relayed Gladys' findings. In his post-war debrief, Spencer had spoken of being buzzed by a craft of immense size, one with no markings, no windows, wings or tail fin. Its speed was silent and spectacular, and Spencer remembered it performing intelligent manoeuvres around the Lancaster before it disappeared into the clouds. It was at that point that their aircraft was attacked by a German night fighter. When the Lancaster caught fire, and the crew ordered to bail out, Spencer had done so successfully. As he floated to Earth, he recalled watching the burning aircraft spiralling to the ground. He also remembered the clouds reflecting a strange green glow and assumed the craft he'd seen earlier had returned.

Spencer's subsequent medical report confirmed that the navigator had suffered severe mental strain during the attack, causing him to hallucinate. The assessment stayed on file. Spencer's written statement had ended up in Nash's burgeoning ranks of locked steel filing cabinets located deep in the bowels of the Air Ministry in Whitehall. As for Spencer, well, he'd died of cancer shortly after the war, taking his secret to the grave.

Through the windshield, Nash watched the sleet turning to cold sheets of rain. So, what to conclude from all of that? Harry Wakefield had witnessed the same thing as Spencer, but had kept quiet. Years later, a similar craft crashes close to his farm and Wakefield is the first on scene. He finds the entity and takes it back to his farmhouse, where it's treated by his wife. What kind of person does that? What kind of person has the wherewithal to encounter something far beyond their understanding yet can act calmly and rationally?

Someone who's had experience with such matters.

Nash cursed under his breath. That moment at Wakefield's door, when he'd looked into the man's eyes, he'd known something was amiss. Ron Chambers had known it too, and the prudent thing would've been to search his property. But they didn't. Standing on that doorstep, Nash had been only a few yards from a living, breathing alien entity, one that was within his grasp, but he'd let it slip through his fingers. Wakefield had bluffed him, successfully, and Nash cursed again.

Phelan's voice crackled from the back seat. Nash reached over and grabbed the handset. 'Go ahead, Syd.'

'Just got a call from the North Wales switchboard, Mister Nash. The car pursuing Wakefield's jeep has just contacted two units approaching from the opposite direction. No sign of Wakefield, or any other vehicle. He must've turned off the road somewhere. He's probably holed up in a farm, maybe an outbuilding or something. I'm running checks to find out if Wakefield or his wife have any relatives or friends in the area.'

Nash keyed the handset. 'Contact Chief Constable Pritchard of the North Wales constabulary. Tell him I want that road blocked and every path and track mapped and searched. I want every door knocked on and every farm, cottage and outbuilding gone over with a fine-tooth comb. I want that vehicle found, and when it is, I want it cordoned off. No one is to go anywhere near it, not until me and Ron get there, understood?'

'Understood,' Phelan echoed, ending the conversation.

Chambers glanced at Nash. 'Shall I turn around?'

Nash shook his head. 'Keep going.'

'Really? What're you thinking?' Chambers asked, his eyes glued to the road as they drove between the shadowy foothills of Snowdonia.

'I'm thinking Wakefield wouldn't go to ground so soon, knowing we'll flood the countryside with police and military units. And why head into Wales at all? The sensible option would've been to head east into England. More roads, larger towns and cities, much easier to get lost. Instead, he drives west, into one of the most sparsely populated areas of the country where the roads are fewer and it's easier for us to close the net.'

'Is that your gut talking again, Mister Nash?'

'It is, Ron. And it's telling me that Wakefield isn't hiding. I think he's heading somewhere.' He leaned over the back seat and scooped up the radio handset. 'Syd, have a couple of unmarked radio cars stake out the Menai Bridge in Bangor. If they spot Wakefield's jeep, have them follow it, discreetly. Nothing else.'

'Roger,' Phelan replied, ending the transmission.

'Bangor it is then,' Chambers said.

'And put your foot down,' Nash told him. 'We may only get one crack at this.'

Chambers flashed his headlights at the police car in front, urging him to pick up the pace. The driver got the message and sped away from the Zephyr, leading the small convoy west, into the dark embrace of the Snowdonia mountains.

ANCIENT ISLE

Harry steered the Land Rover through the quiet, suburban streets of Bangor, avoiding the main routes that led towards the island of Anglesey.

But they couldn't avoid them forever. Their final destination lay another twenty miles distant, along the rugged north-western coast, but first they had to cross the bridge, one that straddled the cold, dark waters of the Menai Strait. Harry could see it now, less than a mile away, its Victorian towers reaching above the rooftops of Bangor and into the starry night sky. The bad weather had chased them all the way to the Snowdonia mountain range, and there it had stopped, allowing them to make good time under clear skies and on dry roads.

'There's the bridge,' Harry told his passengers.

'Vela says we should keep going. He says bad men are chasing us, but he can't tell if they're near or far.'

'How does Vela know that?' Beth asked.

There was silence for a moment, then Charlie said, 'They're using radios. Vela can hear some of their transmissions, like distant church bells carried on the wind. He says they've mentioned our names.'

Harry and Beth shared a look. The further and faster west they'd travelled, the more confident they'd started to feel that they'd left trouble behind them. Now they knew differently.

'If they know we're this far west, they'll assume we're headed for Anglesey,' Beth said. 'Maybe they think we're going to Holyhead, taking a ferry to Ireland?'

Harry slowed as the traffic backed up towards the bridge. 'Maybe. They'll be watching the port anyway, as a precaution, but if they think that's what we're doing, all the better for us.'

They rolled up behind a slow-moving container lorry and turned onto the bridge, moving at a steady fifteen miles per hour, crossing the dark channel of water as it funnelled between the mainland and Anglesey Island. They reached the other side and followed the traffic north, skirting the western edge of town until they approached a busy roundabout. Harry saw signposts for the ferry at Holyhead. Most of the traffic was turning left at the roundabout and heading towards the distant port. He heard Charlie's voice behind him.

'Take the road that goes straight on, Dad.'

Harry did so, driving until they reached the edge of town and the countryside opened up before them. The road was quiet, the traffic almost non-existent now.

'What's this place called again?' Beth asked, tracing her finger on a map she'd retrieved from the glove box and spread across her knees. In the other hand she held a torch.

Harry leaned over and stabbed a finger on the map. 'Carmel Head. It's up there in the north-west corner of the island.'

Beth studied the roads and contours. 'There's hardly anything there. No houses, nothing.'

'The gateway is there,' Charlie said, poking his head around the curtain. 'It's not far now, but we should hurry. Vela just heard another transmission, somewhere behind us. They're coming, Mum. We need to get there before they do.'

Harry turned his head. 'Sit down, Charlie, there's a good lad.'

The boy did as he was told. Harry floored the accelerator, the jeep picking up speed as it hurtled through the night towards the unseen rocky coast.

'Where are they?'

There was a burst of static and then a voice said, 'Heading north-west. They've just picked up the pace.'

'Not the ferry port, then?' Nash asked over the radio.

'Negative. There's not much between them and the coast, a couple of isolated farms and hamlets.'

'Stay on them, but keep your lights off as long as possible. Let's not give the game away just yet.'

'Received,' the voice said.

Chambers glanced at Nash. 'These Welsh coppers seem to know what they're doing.'

'Lucky for us,' Nash agreed. 'How far behind them are we?'

'We're twelve miles short of the Menai Bridge. I'd say an hour, maybe a touch more.'

Nash could see the orange wash of Bangor's lights in the distance. 'What assets do we have on Anglesey?'

'RAF Valley is located on the west coast, just south of

Holyhead. There's also a Royal Navy dock at Holyhead. They've got a couple of search and rescue boats.'

Nash got on the radio to Phelan, who relayed a message to Gladys back in London. Soon the base commander at RAF Valley would get a phone call from the Chief of Defence Staff, who would order him to make preparations to receive a VIP party and transport them via aircraft to RAF Machrihanish in Scotland. Nash's name would be given to the base commander who would be ordered to extend to Nash every professional courtesy, including a detachment of RAF Regiment soldiers placed at Nash's disposal.

As the Zephyr crested another hill, Bangor appeared in the distance. Traffic was light now, the rush-hour long behind them, and they made good time to the bridge. The local constabulary had already cleared a route, and the Ford weaved behind the wailing police car as they crossed the bridge into Anglesey. A few minutes later they were driving past the outskirts of town and into the countryside. Nash reached for the radio and called up Phelan.

'Syd, get on to the base commander at RAF Valley and get those soldiers on the move. Tell them to head north-west. We'll link up with them via radio.'

Phelan acknowledged the request, and the transmission ended. Nash looked through the rear window, saw Hughes' jeep trailing close behind. The game was afoot, and they were closing in. The more Nash studied the map, the more he realised that the escapees had nowhere to go.

His heart began to beat a little faster. With good planning and a little luck, he would soon have a living entity from another world in his custody. Once that happened, the entity, along with the Wakefields, would be transported north to Scotland. At that point Nash will have completed his mission, and his reputation for successful alien craft recovery cemented in the minds of those who wielded enormous power and influence.

The inner circle beckoned.

After that, who knew what lay ahead?

WORM HOLE

THE VESSEL DRIFTED a thousand feet above the earth's surface, black against the cosmos, its hull reflecting the radiance of the planet below it. Its power plant pulsed as it began to orbit slowly, moving across the Californian coast and out over the vast blue expanse of the Pacific Ocean. Ahead lay the Asian landmass, and moments later it slipped beneath the nose of the giant vessel as it headed towards the terminator line.

Far below, day became night, and distant, primitive cities revealed themselves as random clusters of dim light, their inhabitants oblivious to the enormous machine far above them, to the eyes that had watched them for thousands of years. The vessel slowed again as it drifted above the continent of Europe, following the curvature of the earth until it settled into a geosynchronous orbit above a collection of jagged rock formations at the edge of the Atlantic Ocean.

Powerful sensors scanned the landmass below, quickly locating a specific electromagnetic signal that emanated from the ground. It was an ancient signal, an acoustic aberration of time and geology, of which there were many such anomalies at sites across the planet, beneath prehistoric pyramids, stone structures and temples, all constructed by primitive peoples who wondered at the magnitude of the heavens and accepted the existence of beings that lived there far more easily than their modern descendants.

The vessel remained motionless, moving in synchronicity with the landmass below. A massive door opened midway along its superstructure and a craft emerged, the black, wingless machine drifting out into space. A moment later its power plant engaged, and it dipped its nose, carving its way through the thickening atmosphere towards the rugged landmass below.

'IT'S THERE, JUST UP AHEAD.'

'You're sure?'

'We are.'

Harry's eyes scanned the darkness. They'd passed through slumbering villages and silent hamlets and had yet to see a living soul. They'd not seen another car for the past five miles. The distant rooftops of scattered houses and farms were behind them now, giving way to a landscape of dark fields, punctuated with trees and hedges bent and twisted by decades of coastal winds. Then Harry saw it, a pair of black metal gates set back in a low stone wall. Beyond the wall, another field and a shadowy border of pine trees.

Harry slowed and turned into the gate. Through the rusted black bars, the Land Rover's headlights picked out a road that twisted across the field and disappeared into the trees.

'Are you sure this is it?'

'Go Dad. Quickly.'

'I'll get the gates,' Beth said, throwing open her door.

Cold air whistled around the Land Rover as Beth swung the rusted gates back against their tall stone pillars. Harry drove in and waited, engine rattling, as Beth closed the gates behind them. Then they were moving, the road cutting across a wide open field before twisting through a thick wood of pines.

'Feels like we're trespassing,' Beth said.

'We'll find out soon enough.'

As they rounded another dark turn, the trees thinned, and the landscape opened up ahead. That's when Harry saw the house.

'Impressive,' he said as the Land Rover's tyres crunched over a gravel drive. The house was a sprawling, period property, the central section of the building book-ended by two wings of equal and impressive size.

'It's a manor house,' Beth observed. 'Looks deserted.'

Harry thought the same. Every visible window was dark, and no lights burned anywhere on the property. Harry stopped the Rover, switched off the engine and climbed out. The main doors were set inside a deep, shadowy porch but no light shone there or anywhere else, including the outbuildings next to the property. On closer inspection the building had a slightly neglected feel to it, the paint around the windows peeling, the lawns and hedges wild and unkempt.

Beth stood next to Harry, her coat wrapped tightly around her. 'What now?'

'Listen.'

The wind gusted across the property, carrying the boom and hiss of the sea. Harry pointed to the open grounds to the side of the house. 'The sea must be just over those bluffs.'

'Harry.'

It was the tone of Beth's voice that made him turn around, and he saw a figure watching them from the shadows of the porch. Harry squinted, but all he could see was a pale, hairless head suspended above a small body in dark clothing. Then the figure stepped out onto the gravel and Harry saw it was an oriental man, bald with a snow-white beard and a slight stoop to his back. He wore a black smock buttoned to the neck, and baggy trousers that rode high above the slippers on his feet. He stopped a few feet away and bowed his head.

'My name is Zhen. I am the custodian of the gateway.' He pointed to the Land Rover. 'The explorer, he is here?' He opened the back door without waiting for an answer.

Zhen chuckled as Charlie scrambled out, and Beth took her son's hand. A moment later, Zhen was helping Vela out of the vehicle. Harry noticed they were of similar proportions, though Vela's head was bigger. Beth stepped closer.

'How's your breathing?' she asked, tapping her chest.

Harry's eyes widened as Vela's lipless mouth moved, and he heard what sounded like a rapid, musical rhyme of chirps and chips.

'He's much better,' Zhen translated. 'He thanks all of you for your help, but the sickness will return soon. We must hurry.'

He looped his arm through Vela's and together they walked towards the house, their footsteps barely disturbing the gravel. Vela held out his hand and Charlie took it. Harry watched them disappear into the shadows of the porch.

'I give up trying to work any of this out,' Beth said to him.

'I gave up a while back.' Harry reached for her empty hand and squeezed it. 'Come on. Whatever's about to happen, I don't want to miss it.'

They hurried across the gravel and into the house.

THE POLICE CAR ahead of them slowed. Nash saw two men stood by an unmarked car at the side of the road. One of them was waving a torch.

'Stop,' Nash ordered.

Chambers stamped on the brakes. Nash climbed out and into a cold wind. He watched the Land Rover pull up behind. They held an impromptu conference in the middle of the deserted road.

'Where are they?' Nash asked the plain-clothed officers.

One of them pointed into the darkness. 'There's a manor house, up there on the right, about a quarter of a mile. There's nothing else on this road, no houses, farms, caravans, nothing.'

'Who lives there?'

'No idea.'

Nash turned to the uniforms. 'Stay here and block this road. There's a military convoy on its way. When it gets here, wave them through. No one else, understood?'

The uniforms nodded. Nash led Chambers and Hughes out of earshot. The surrounding land was windswept and desolate, and he could taste the tang of salt on the air. He spoke to Hughes first.

'Frank, wait here for the soldiers. When they get here, double them up to the property on foot. We'll meet you there.'

'Right you are,' Hughes said, and jogged back to the jeep.

Nash watched him go, then turned and looked into the distance. There were no lights anywhere, but the wind was keeping the sky clear and visibility was good.

'What d'you suppose they're doing here?' Chambers asked.

'Trying to lie low would be my guess. It's remote, quiet, no other buildings for at least a mile in any direction. They probably think they're safe, which is good news for us because their guard will be down.'

'Wakefield's a tough customer,' Chambers warned. 'He's armed too. There could be trouble.'

Nash shook his head. 'Not with his wife and son in tow. He'll do as he's told.' He thrust his hands in his pockets as the wind picked up, gusting across the surrounding fields.

'So, what's the plan?' Chambers asked.

'You and I will go up and quietly check the property. As soon as Hughes and the troops arrive, we'll throw a cordon around the place and move in. With a little luck, we should have this all wrapped up pretty soon.'

'Sounds good,' Chambers said, rubbing his hands together. 'I've had just about enough of running around Wales in the middle of winter.'

'Ditto,' Nash echoed. 'Come on, let's go take a look.'

The men set off, their backs bowed against the wind as they headed into the darkness.

GATEWAY

THEY FOLLOWED Zhen through the house, the oil lamp in his hand spilling light across stone floors, stuffed furniture and wall paintings. Watching Charlie holding Vela's hand, Harry felt strangely excluded from proceedings. He gave Beth's hand a squeeze, and she glanced at him with worried eyes. A large door opened up before them and they filed inside a huge kitchen where a fire crackled and spat in a granite fireplace. Zhen closed the door, then he turned to them and bowed.

'It is an honour to meet you, Harry and Elizabeth Wakefield. And young Charlie, of course.'

Harry was baffled. 'How d'you know our names.'

'Vela told him,' Charlie explained.

'But how d'you know if—'

'Please,' Zhen interrupted. 'We have little time, and there are things our friend and I must discuss.' He waved a hand at the kitchen table. 'Please, help yourselves to tea. We will return shortly.'

They left the room by another door. Harry sat Charlie

down and passed him a packet of biscuits. He poured tea for all of them from a warm pot.

'This gets more bizarre with every minute,' Beth said, sipping her brew.

'I know.' Harry smiled at his son. 'How are you, Charlie? How are you feeling?'

'I know you're scared,' Charlie smiled, 'but you don't have to be, Dad. Vela knows what he's doing.'

'I'm not scared, Son. I need to know you're okay, that's all.'

Beth turned in her chair and held her son's face in her hands. 'All this stuff that's happened, it can be confusing, maybe a little scary, but your Dad and I will always be here for you. That's our job, to make sure you're safe and happy. If there's anything you want to say, anything you're upset about, you need to tell us.'

Charlie's chubby face beamed. 'I'm fine, Mum. You mustn't worry.'

'You realise you can't go with Vela. You know that, don't you? None of us can go.'

That's when it hit Harry. Beth had already seen the danger, and now Harry saw it too. What if Vela tried to take Charlie with him? Worse still, what if Charlie wanted to go? He'd become attached to Vela, both physically and mentally, and Charlie had changed since they'd met. He was...*normal*, Harry realised. What would happen when Vela left? Would Charlie revert back to his old self? As Harry's stomach churned, Charlie answered his Mum.

'I know I can't go,' he said, smiling. 'I don't want to, not unless we all go. Maybe sometime in the future.'

'Maybe,' Beth said, her eyes moist. She squeezed him tight, and he squeezed her back, and the panic bubbling in Harry's gut subsided. They drank their tea in silence, but

Harry knew the lull wouldn't last long, and his mind began to consider the next few days. They would be very tough, perhaps devastating, for all of them.

Vela and Zhen returned several minutes later. 'It's time to go,' the Oriental said. 'There are men at the gate. Soon others will arrive.'

Beth paled in the firelight. 'How did they find us?'

'It is irrelevant,' Zhen told them. 'All that matters is departure. Come, we should head to the gateway.'

'Wait,' Harry said, looking at Vela. 'The night I fell from the plane I saw a ship, just like the one you came here in. Something happened to me that night, but I can't explain it. I should've died. Please, help me understand.'

Vela whistled and chirped for a few seconds. Zhen listened, nodding, then he filled in the blanks. 'The destruction of your aircraft was witnessed, and your fall prevented. You were examined, marked for monitoring, then released into the snowdrift. Now, we must leave.'

Harry stood in his way. 'Wait, what does that mean?'

'It means you are of interest,' Zhen told him, his face darkening. 'Do not question it, Mister Wakefield, just accept it for what it is. You will sleep easier.'

Harry stared at Vela. 'At least tell me where you're from. Please.'

Vela cocked his head, as if he were considering the request, then he raised his hand. A bright white square appeared in the air, floating just above the kitchen table. It was just like the one Vela showed them back at the house. It crackled with interference for a moment, and then it sharpened to an image, a moving one...

And they were flying above a savannah of tall, purple grass. Below them, green zebra-like creatures galloped in a mighty herd, and then they were gone, left far behind as they flew across a huge forest of such vivid colours that it nearly took Harry's breath away. And then he saw it, rising up in the distance, a gleaming city, ringed by mountains and built upon the shores of a vast, blue lake. They flew closer, and they saw giant spires of glass and crystal reaching up into the sky, and domes of such magnificence that Harry gripped Beth's hand, as if he were riding a roller-coaster. Instead, he was flying above a city of such size and beauty that he felt an uncontrollable wave of emotion threatening to engulf him. Then the image faded. Harry reeled as if he'd been punched. He dropped to his knees and held Charlie's shoulders.

'You knew, didn't you? That was your drawing, in your colouring book, wasn't it? You'd seen it before.'

'In my dreams,' Charlie said, smiling. 'I told you the grass was purple.'

'You were right, Son.' Harry held the boy tight, tears stinging his eyes.

He felt a hand on his shoulder, and Vela looked down at him, his eyes blinking, his mouth chirping and clicking.

'You must forgive him, but he has to leave now,' the custodian translated.

Harry straightened up. 'Let's go.'

Zhen led the way, through the kitchen and out through a set of glass doors. They crossed a stone patio, then a lawn bordered by low hedges. There was no moon, but the sky was cold and clear and visibility was fair. It improved a little as they cleared the hedges and walked into a field at the back of the house. He heard waves crashing against the shore, louder now, and the ground sloped away to the nearby bluffs. Beyond them, Harry saw whitecaps in the darkness. Then he noticed something else, a circle of stone obelisks arranged in the surrounding field. Zhen brought them to a halt at the edge of the circle. It was an ancient monument, Harry realised, one of those archaeological places of significance from a time far back in history. Harry took a few steps towards the closest one and touched it. It was about twelve feet tall, heavy and solid, yet smooth to the touch, its granite surface weathered by time and the elements.

'What is this place?'

'This is the gateway,' Zhen explained. 'Vela's people have been visiting this planet for millennia. This place, just one of many, possesses a strong magnetic vibration that can be seen and felt for vast distances. The explorers use them for guidance and calibration. Occasionally for extraction.'

Vela was standing next to Zhen, his big eyes blinking, his lipless mouth formed into what Harry thought was a smile.

'I have so many questions, I don't know where to start.'

'There's no time,' Zhen told him.

Harry took a step closer. He pointed to the sky and said to Vela, 'Which one is yours?'

Vela raised an arm and extended a slender finger. Above their heads, reaching far across the night sky, was a hazy carpet of suffused light littered with stars, some bright, others faint, a tapestry of celestial wonder that had transfixed mankind since the beginning of time.

'The Milky Way,' Zhen told them, 'a galaxy that contains our own Solar System, yet its sheer magnitude has yet to be realised. One day our scientists will discover that it contains almost four-hundred billion stars and a hundred million planets, many of them like our own.'

Zhen pointed to a vague cluster of light directly overhead.

'Vela's home is there, twenty-eight light-years away.

Long ago his people mastered the technology to travel across the galaxy. In that time they have visited many worlds and many civilisations. They have been coming here before mankind was able to walk upright.'

'Unbelievable,' Beth whispered, her head tilted towards the heavens.

Harry's eyes travelled across the vastness of space above him, and he struggled to comprehend what Zhen was telling them. He thought about Vela's world, and the other worlds he must've seen, the other races and civilisations, and suddenly Harry felt as insignificant as the smallest of God's creatures.

Vela chirped. Zhen smiled in the darkness and pointed. 'They're here.'

Harry gripped Beth and Charlie's hands and looked towards the bluffs. The wind whipped around them, and then Harry saw it, a faint green glow moving across the surface of the sea. It got brighter as it closed the distance, and then the glow lit up the bluffs and crossed the field towards them. That's when Harry saw it, barely visible against the night sky, but its sheer blackness gave it shape and substance. *A ship*, just like the one up on Craggan Peak, moving silently towards them. *Not silent,* Harry realised. He detected a very faint hum, and Harry stepped backwards, taking Beth and Charlie with him as the ship rotated in the air above them and came to a silent stop directly above the stone circle. It lit up the ancient monument in a soft green glow.

Harry smiled. 'Are you seeing this,' he whispered. 'Amazing. Absolutely fantastic.' He was no longer scared, he realised. He felt elated, almost giddy. The sheer wonder of it all was nothing short of miraculous, and suddenly

Harry didn't want it to end, didn't want to return to his old life.

Vela's head swivelled. Zhen said, 'the government people are here. There isn't much time.'

Vela stepped forward and put his hand on Charlie's face. He chirped something, and Charlie nodded and smiled. Vela's black eyes blinked once, and then he walked into the middle of the stone circle. A narrow shaft of white light enveloped him and a moment later he was levitating up towards a bright square of light beneath the craft. He disappeared from view a moment later, and the shaft of light blinked out.

That's when Harry heard the shout behind him.

DANGER CLOSE

'HELP ME WITH THE GATES, QUICKLY!'

Nash and Chambers took one each and swung them open. They screeched on rusty hinges and Nash hurried back out to the road and waved Hughes through the gates, along with a platoon of soldiers from RAF Valley. They waited in a large, puffing group, their breath clouding on the cold air. Nash pointed to the distant pine forest.

'Once we hit the trees, split left and right and surround the property, make sure no one escapes.'

Hughes nodded and ordered the troops to follow him at the double. Nash and Chambers ran behind them as boots and shoes pounded the tarmac all the way to the tree-line. Hughes waved them left and right, his orders coming in frantic whispers. Nash watched them fanning out through the trees, weaving quietly towards the shadowy rooftops of the distant house. Nash and Chambers pushed on, running along the tarmac, Browning pistols in their hands. Their shoes crunched on gravel, any element of stealth now gone. Nash headed straight for the porch. He tried twisting the door's large metal handle, but it held firm.

He pounded on it with a fist, but his efforts sounded frail against the door's thickness. Forcing entry wasn't an option here.

'Round the back,' Nash ordered, waving his gun. Chambers led the way, spraying gravel as they rounded the corner of the house and plunged into the darkness of the surrounding gardens. They vaulted low hedges as Nash followed Chambers towards a wide stone patio at the back of the house. The wind was stronger now, and brought with it the sound of breaking waves from a nearby shore. Faint orange light spilled across the patio. Chambers kept low, creeping towards the French doors, with Nash close behind. He stopped at the doors and peered around the edge. Nash stepped in front of him and looked.

He saw a huge kitchen, lit only by a fire in a stone hearth. There was no one in there, no movement in the shadows. He noticed mugs and a teapot on the table, an open tin of biscuits. There were chairs at scattered angles, hurriedly abandoned. He reached out for the handle, forced it down slowly. It moved easily. He cracked the door open—

'Wait,' Chambers hissed. 'Look.'

Nash turned and followed Chambers' pointed finger, through the silhouettes of bushes and trees to the sloping field beyond—to the hovering craft, to the pencil-thin shaft of light that probed the stone circle below it. To the figures that stood watching.

The shaft of light blinked out.

The stone circle glowed green.

'Come on!'

ZHEN RAISED his arms and smiled, as if he were waving relatives off on a cruise ship. The craft drifted across the stone circle, the ground lit up by that strange green glow, and then it was over the bluffs and heading out to sea.

'Stop! Nobody move!'

Harry heard the shout behind him, and he pulled Beth and Charlie behind one of the stone obelisks. Two men appeared out of the darkness, clutching hand guns, their overcoats flapping behind them. Harry raised his hands, and then he recognised Nash and his heavy sidekick running towards them, but the Ministry man ignored Harry and ran past him, through the stone circle and out towards the bluffs. Then he stopped and lowered his gun, and they all watched the craft moving out to sea, lighting up the surface beneath its fat body. And then it sped away, and the glow disappeared towards the dark horizon. Harry watched Nash as the man stood motionless, his shoulders slumped, staring out to sea.

'Stay here,' Harry whispered to Beth and Charlie. He glanced at the heavy who stood open-mouthed, then walked out towards Nash. He stood next to him, the wind gusting around them, the sky dark and empty.

'He's gone.'

Nash nodded, and then he turned around. The gun was still in his hand, dangling by his side, and Harry was having trouble gauging Nash's mood. He thought it hovered somewhere between anger and bitter disappointment. Either way, it didn't bode well for the rest of them.

'Gun,' he demanded, his hand waiting. Harry pulled the Luger from his belt and handed it over. 'You're in a lot of trouble, Wakefield. You and your family.'

Harry shook his head. 'This is nothing to do with them, they're just bystanders in all this. I'm the one who's responsible. And I'd appreciate it if you kept the gun out of sight. They're frightened enough already.'

Nash stared at him from beneath the brim of his hat, and then he pulled his coat open and jammed his gun into a shoulder holster. 'Happy?'

'Thank you.' Harry took a deep breath and let it out slowly. 'So, what happens now?'

'We take a little trip. To Scotland.'

Harry's stomach churned. 'What's in Scotland?'

Nash offered a hard, humourless smile. 'You know the drill, Wakefield. Your mission is over, so it's time for a debrief. And there are people who'd like to speak with you, important people.' He looked over Harry's shoulder and shouted into the darkness. 'Ron, tell Frank to bring the transport here now.' Nash cocked his chin at the small figure standing next to Beth and Charlie. 'Who's that?'

Harry shrugged. 'No idea.'

Nash stared at him with cold eyes.

'Not a good start, Harry. Not a good start at all.'

CHARLIE SPENT most of the flight looking out of the window, although Harry knew there wasn't much to see apart from a few pinpricks of light dotted around the black horizon. It kept the boy preoccupied however, and Harry watched Beth coo reassuringly in his ear as they huddled beneath a blanket.

Harry sat behind them, across the narrow aisle. Zhen was up near the cockpit, a burly soldier wedged into the aisle seat next to him. Nash had split them up, maybe because the Ministry man was worried about them concocting a story or some other nonsense. Harry was past caring, such was his exhaustion. All that mattered now was his family, particularly Charlie. The boy was probably hurting, but Beth would have to stand in for both of them in the short term. Harry's focus had to be getting them out of this mess.

Their escort party occupied the other seats of the de Havilland Heron transporter; Nash and his two black-suited colleagues (*Chambers* and *Phelan* he discovered), plus three soldiers in maroon berets and a cap badge that

Harry didn't recognise. Nash referred to the officer as *Hughes,* a cold individual whose unblinking stare made Harry a little uncomfortable. These were serious people, he knew that much. Best not to upset them.

No one spoke as the plane headed north, a bumpy flight that took them out over the Irish Sea. Harry estimated they were travelling at around twelve thousand feet, evidenced by glimpses of civilisation beneath the starboard wing; the town of Douglas on the Isle of Man, and the port of Stranraer on the Scottish coast, by Harry's reckoning. Western Scotland, then. What lay in store for them, God only knew.

A short time later he saw Nash walk up to the cockpit. There was a brief conversation with the pilots, then he returned to the cabin and started closing the window blinds. Chambers, Phelan and Hughes helped complete the task, and the aircraft began to descend. Harry wasn't used to landing blind like that, and when the wheels hit the tarmac thirty minutes later it came as a relief. The de Havilland taxied for several minutes, twisting and turning along unseen taxiways, and then Harry heard the propellers roar, the sound amplified by a noticeable echo. *We're in a hangar,* he realised. A few moments later and the aircraft jerked to a stop. The engines wound down, and Nash walked past him and cracked the bulkhead door. Then he ordered everyone to leave the aircraft.

Harry deplaned behind Beth and Charlie, the steps outside illuminated by faceless shadows holding torches. The hangar they stood in was the biggest he'd ever seen, made even more enormous because the giant space was unlit, and appeared to be empty. Clanking metal hammered the walls, and Harry watched the massive hangar doors rattling closed. He glimpsed the world outside, but saw nothing more than a string of distant lights. *A perimeter fence*, he guessed. That, and glimpses of RAF uniforms around him told Harry he was on an airbase in western Scotland, but which one? Turnberry? Prestwick perhaps?

'Where are we?' Harry asked.

'No talking.'

Shadowy escorts led the way around the nose of the de Havilland, their torches probing the gloom. Harry held Beth and Charlie's hands as a concrete wall loomed. Torch beams picked out a set of double doors, and on the other side was a well-lit corridor. A huge one, Harry saw, clearly mirroring the depth of the hangar they'd just left, but it was stark and featureless, lacking any signage on its concrete walls. It reminded Harry of a bomb shelter, apart from the coloured lines painted on the floor that led into the distance. Charlie skipped over them, his booted feet hopping from colour to colour, as if this were all a game. Harry imagined that's all it was for his son, an exciting, wonderful adventure that he probably didn't want to end. Harry remembered feeling the same back on Anglesey. He didn't feel like that anymore.

Marching ahead, Nash turned another corner, and the party followed. Halfway down another long, empty corridor, he called a halt outside an open steel door. Beyond was a small room, with a bunk and a tiny sink. Like a prison cell.

'This is you,' Nash said, nodding at Harry.

'Me?'

'Just you,' Nash confirmed.

Harry swallowed hard. The game just got a lot darker. He squeezed Beth and Charlie's hands. 'We're staying together.'

Hughes took a step forward, his hard eyes drilling into him. Nash gave Harry the smallest shake of his head. 'Don't make a scene, Harry, there's a good chap. For the boy's sake.'

'We'll be fine,' Beth told him, pulling her hand free.

'Come on, Charlie, let's go with the nice man.' She gave Harry a tight smile, and her eyes begged him to cooperate.

Harry stepped inside the room, the walls and floor made of the same grey concrete. There was a thin, faded rug next to the bed and a toilet behind a curtain rail.

'Wait, I need to—'

The door slammed behind him, and Harry saw there was no handle on the inside. It really was a cell. Panic swirled inside his chest, and he thumped a futile fist on the door.

'Don't worry, Beth, it'll be alright!' he shouted, but the echo of his voice mocked him. The truth was, he had no idea if any of them would be alright.

Or what would happen next.

It had taken almost fifteen hours for the convoy to reach the gates of RAF Machrihanish, and Corporal Billy Stone had to admit that he was pretty exhausted. It'd been a long haul up the west coast of the country, and while travelling at night had its advantages—in this case minimal exposure of their convoy—it also required a lot more concentration, which took its toll both mentally *and* physically. He'd taken turns with Ernie, swapping places to drive the truck, but there was only so much rest a man could expect in the draughty cab of a noisy transport truck. When the miles had ticked down, and the base had finally appeared out of a fine coastal mist, both Billy and Ernie were glad to see it.

After rumbling along a road next to an endless perimeter fence, Billy revved the engine and geared the big beast down. Up ahead, one of the escort jeeps was parked at an angle across the road, and two RAF military policemen were waving the truck through one of the smaller and more remote access gates at the far end of the base. Billy checked his mirrors and threw the wheel around, once again giving silent thanks that their load, despite its mass, weighed next to nothing. *Bloody amazing,* Ernie had said when he'd first driven the Antar. And it was. The whole operation was.

But she was big, her black nose sticking out over the front of the cab, her fat arse hovering far beyond the tail-lights, her waist hanging out on either side of the truck. *The Martian Hindenburg,* Ernie called it, and they'd both laughed.

Billy steered the rig through the open chain-link gates, where armed soldiers in wet-weather gear waved them onwards. There was a portable metal sign on the road in front of them—*TURN OFF LIGHTS*—and Billy did so, looking to his right and the far end of the runway. Beyond the tarmac, the cliffs gave way to a grey, empty sea.

As escort vehicles shepherded them like pilot fish, Billy eased the rig along an access road that ran parallel to the runway, the longest either of them had ever seen. It stretched far into the distance, and they briefly discussed what sort of aircraft might need such a long runway. A jeep swept past them, the passenger waving them to follow him. It was the American, Fisk, and Billy gave him a thumbs-up.

They drove past grass-covered hardened shelters and nondescript brick buildings with numbers instead of signs. They didn't see a single aircraft, and Billy guessed that the weather had put paid to flight operations. And to nosy park-ers. They saw the control tower in the distance, but it came and went as the coastal mist lingered over the base.

Then Ernie pointed through the windshield. 'Bloody hell, that's a big 'un.'

Billy saw it then, across the runway, a giant hangar that

loomed out of the mist, and he followed Fisk's jeep all the way to its huge sliding doors. The roar of the Antar's engine echoed across the vast cavern, and Billy kept well clear of the small transport plane parked in a dark corner. Fisk's jeep looped around in a wide circle and Billy followed him until their vehicles were facing the hangar doors. Brake lights blazed in the gloom. Billy stamped on the pedal and brought the rig to a stop in a loud hiss of air brakes.

'At last,' Ernie said, yawning. 'I could murder a cup of tea and a bacon sandwich.'

'Let's do a visual first.'

Billy jumped down, stretching his limbs. He walked around the load, checking for any loose straps, chains and broken strong points. He ducked under the tail of the thing, passing Ernie as they double-checked each other's inspection. Billy met Fisk up by the nose. Rain water poured off the tarpaulins and pooled on the concrete floor.

'All secure, sir.'

'Good job,' Fisk nodded.

Billy looked up at the belly of the craft that hung over their heads. 'If you don't mind me asking, what happens to her now?'

'She's going on a trip,' the American said, but he didn't elaborate.

Billy knew when to keep his mouth shut. 'Do you mind if me and Ernie get some breakfast?'

Fisk nodded. 'Sure thing. You guys relax, take it easy. I'll send for you when the time comes.'

Billy walked away and Ernie fell in beside him. An RAF policeman pointed them to a distant door, and as they walked across the hangar, they heard a deep rumbling. Behind them, the giant doors were closing, shutting out the daylight with an impressive *boom*.

'I suggest we have ourselves a good feed and a smoke, then try to get our heads down somewhere,' Billy said.

Ernie rubbed his hands together. 'Sounds like a plan, Billy-boy.' He cocked a thumb over his shoulder and said, 'We've done some things in our time, but this takes the biscuit, eh? Something to tell the grandkids one day.'

Billy put an arm around his Co-driver and pulled him close. 'You know the drill, Ernie. You open your mouth about this to anyone, ever, and you'll be signing your own death warrant.'

Ernie winced. 'C'mon, Bill. You know I was only joking.'

'You must've been,' Billy smiled, slapping Ernie's back. 'Now, let's see about that breakfast, eh?'

THE DOOR SWUNG OPEN. Hughes waited outside with two soldiers. He beckoned Harry into the corridor.

'Let's go.'

Harry didn't argue. He was relieved to be out of that cold, cramped cell, and desperate to see his family. The soldiers said nothing as they strode along the corridor, their boots squeaking on the concrete floor. As they approached an intersection, Harry saw some figures ahead. More soldiers, he realised. Except one. The young man in their midst.

'Colin!'

Hughes spun around and stood an inch from Harry's nose. 'Not another word,' he snarled. By the time Hughes stepped away, Colin was gone.

They escorted Harry into a large hall that was almost universally grey; a smooth grey concrete floor, bare grey walls, a high, grey ceiling festooned with grey-painted pipes.

Long-drop lights with grey shades threw the surrounding walls into shadow. Harry couldn't work out what the space might normally be used for; a warehouse perhaps, or a sports hall, but today it was being used for something else. Something far from normal.

Hughes and his square-jawed soldiers escorted him to the middle of the hall where a single wooden chair had been placed in front of a long table. Sitting behind that table, three suited men watched Harry with inquisitive eyes. They were all in their fifties, their dark-blue suits tailored, their shirt collars white and stiff, their ties knotted perfectly. *Politicians*, was Harry's initial guess, but he didn't recognise any of them. Would the Prime Minister send low-level civil servants for such an event? Probably not. *Military* in that case, in civilian clothes. Whoever they were they reeked of power, so Harry sat down and said nothing. The stamp of standard-issue boots receded. A door slammed, echoing around the hall.

The man in the middle cleared his throat. He had a sharp, angular face and a hooked nose that he held high, staring down its bony ridge at Harry. When he spoke his voice filled the hall, his words clipped and authoritative.

'My name is Goodman. My colleagues and I have some questions.'

'I need to see my family,' Harry told them. 'It's been over twenty-four hours. I need to know they're okay.'

'Your wife and son are perfectly safe,' Goodman told him.

'I want to see them, right now.'

'That won't be possible, not until we finish our session.'

Harry folded his arms. 'In that case, I'm not saying another word.'

There was silence behind the table as the men studied

him with cold eyes. Finally Goodman said, 'Are you a patriot, Mister Wakefield?'

Harry stiffened. 'Of course I am. What sort of question is that?'

'A perfectly reasonable one. You see, the war years are behind us now, and while fascism has been defeated, the infinitely more dangerous scourge of communism has taken its place. Some of our fellow countrymen have been seduced by its ideology and strive to create a political bridgehead in Britain for their Soviet masters. In short, enemy forces are operating here, on our shores.'

Harry frowned. 'I don't follow.'

'We are at war, Mister Wakefield. Thankfully, not a shooting war, but a conflict on every other level—militarily, politically, economically, socially. Advances in science and technology play a huge part in this quiet conflict. For example, the Russians are ahead in the space race. Our American cousins are doing their level best to close that gap, but the domination of Earth's upper atmosphere and beyond is now a priority for the west.'

Goodman's chair creaked as he leaned forward.

'You have been exposed to a phenomenon, Mister Wakefield, one that will tip the balance of global power in the favour of those who can master its technology. A phenomenon that is publicly ridiculed by western governments, yet quietly acknowledged as the most critical issue of our time. A phenomenon considered far more important than our nuclear deterrent. Do you see where I'm headed with all this, Mister Wakefield?'

Harry frowned. 'I'm not sure.'

'It means that, given the highly sensitive nature of the incident at Craggan Peak—and your involvement in it—I can have you and your family detained indefinitely. Do you understand?'

Harry's stomach twisted with a knot of fear. Whoever these men were, they operated in a world far beyond anything he'd known before. He swallowed hard and offered Goodman a submissive nod. The man behind the table smiled.

'I have no wish to threaten or intimidate, Mister Wakefield. My only aim here is to explore the facts. Now, I have spoken to your wife and son and they have cooperated fully. Do the same and we shall reunite you with them when we are done. On that you have my word.'

Harry's heart thumped inside his chest. He sat a little straighter in his chair.

'What is it you want to know?'

Goodman glanced at a file on the table in front of him. 'Your recent encounter with a craft of unknown origin was not your first, was it, Mister Wakefield?'

Harry shook his head. 'I saw something very similar during the war.'

'The night you were shot down, correct? When you fell eighteen thousand feet without a parachute. And survived.'

'Yes. It buzzed us, just before we were attacked by a German night fighter.'

'Yet you failed to mention this in your subsequent debrief. Why?'

Harry shrugged. 'I knew other people who'd reported them. There was a lot of ridicule, and some of them were grounded for one reason or another. I wanted to keep flying, so I kept my mouth shut.'

'I see you were declared medically unfit after the war,' Goodman noted. 'Occasional blackouts, sleepwalking episodes.'

Harry's fingers touched the side of his head. It was reflex gesture. 'It started when I got back to England. It didn't happen often, maybe once every few months, but I found myself waking up in different rooms around the house. Then it happened at work a couple of times. I'd be in another area of the factory, but I couldn't remember how I got there.'

'This is the car factory in Nottingham. Where you met your wife.'

Harry nodded. 'She treated me after a fall I couldn't remember. They let me go after that, told me I was an accident waiting to happen.' The look on Goodman's face told him something else. 'You know something, don't you?'

'Not much,' Goodman admitted. 'Although we believe the blackouts are somehow related to encounters with these beings.'

He watched one of the other men lean into Goodman's ear and whisper something. Goodman nodded and turned his attention back to Harry.

'Let's focus on recent events, shall we? Can you tell us why you failed to report the presence of the living entity?'

Harry shifted in his chair. 'I don't know. I guess I wasn't thinking.'

'Did you consider the risk of contamination, Mister Wakefield?'

'I don't follow.'

Goodman toyed with a pen as he lectured Harry like a schoolboy. 'When Spanish explorers landed in Mexico in the sixteenth century, they brought a myriad of diseases with them; smallpox, influenza, other Old World viruses. Indigenous immune systems could not cope with such a biological onslaught and died by the hundreds of thousands. Using that same theory, a single alien entity has the potential to introduce an unstoppable pathogen that could wipe out the entire human race. A very real and dangerous scenario, wouldn't you agree?'

Harry's stomach lurched as he remembered carrying Vela in his arms. And Beth treating his wounds. Holding Charlie's hand. 'I didn't think of that.'

'What *did* you think of?'

Harry shrugged. 'Nothing. I was in a state of shock, just seeing that ship sitting up there on the peak. And when I saw him—'

'Vela,' Goodman interrupted, referring to the document in front of him. 'That's what you called the being, yes?'

'He said his name was unpronounceable.'

'And he communicated telepathically?'

'For a while. Beth and I suffered headaches and bleeding.'

'But not your son.'

Harry shook his head. 'No. For some reason he's able to cope, although long term—'

'Your son has been examined thoroughly,' Goodman assured him. 'He's in perfect health, and rather wilful I might add. He gave us quite a ticking off.'

Harry almost smiled. Almost. 'My wife and son, they had nothing to do with this. I made all the decisions. They had no choice but to go along with it. They're innocent.'

Goodman interlocked his slender fingers. 'Let me be clear, Mister Wakefield, this is not a police matter. You are not in any trouble—'

'I shot two men with an unregistered firearm. I ran from the police.'

'Those matters are of no concern. You're not on trial here. This is merely an information-gathering exercise, to record your experience. One that even you will admit is barely believable.'

Harry raised an eyebrow. 'What do you mean, *even you*?'

Goodman smiled. 'I'm referring to your fall.'

It was several moments before Harry spoke again. He'd never really considered telling anyone the truth of what happened that night, and by the time he'd met Beth years later, he'd buried the memory. Now it was time to dig it up.

He closed his eyes for a moment, and then he was back in that turret, looking down at his sheepskin jacket, at the smoke swirling around his boots, the flames licking close by. He heard the screams of his crew. His friends...

'I was terrified. One way or another, I knew I would die, but I didn't want to burn to death. So I jumped. The plane was falling too, right next to me, burning, engines screaming, spinning like a top. I had trouble breathing, and I wanted it to be over. Then I saw it burst out of a cloud above me, nose down, heading in my direction, and for a second I forgot about dying. Then I blacked out. I woke up in that snowdrift hours later.'

The men listened silently. Harry could feel his heart beating in his chest.

'And what did you deduce from that experience?'

'That somehow they caught me, set me down on the ground. I don't know how or why, I just know. They saved me, so when Vela asked me for help, my first instinct was to return the favour.'

Goodman tapped his pen on the table, lost in thought for several moments. Finally he spoke. 'You are the first human being ever to have spent considerable time in the company of a live entity, Mister Wakefield. Had my organisation had such an opportunity, we might've learned a great deal.'

'By making him prisoner?'

'By communicating.'

'I got the impression he wasn't keen on talking to anyone in authority. He just wanted to get back to his people.'

'Did he say why his ship crashed?'

Harry shrugged. 'He mentioned something—anti-matter displacement, something like that. Something failed. He didn't elaborate. I think he saw me go cross-eyed and gave up.'

Goodman had another brief, whispered discussion. Pens scratched across paper. When Goodman spoke again, his voice was thick with disappointment.

'We could've learned so much from him. Still, he left us quite a haul. Hardware *and* bodies. We must be grateful for that, at least.' Goodman refocused and clicked his pen. 'Did he give any indication as to where he was from?'

'Somewhere in the Milky Way,' Harry told him. 'Twenty-eight light-years from Earth, he said.'

'A life-supporting planet in our own galaxy?' said the man to Goodman's left. It was the first time he'd spoken, and Harry nodded in the affirmative.

'Not just one. Vela said there were millions. Just like Earth.'

His interrogators huddled together as they entered into an indecipherable conversation. Harry got the impression they were hearing that information for the very first time. Goodman cleared his throat.

'The Chinaman, Zhen,' he asked Harry. 'What was his role in all of this?'

'I've no idea. He was as shocked as us.'

'So it would seem. It appears to have rendered him speechless. We've only managed to get a few words out of him, and according to our linguists, they're in an ancient dialect of Mandarin.'

'Poor bloke,' Harry said, and meant it.

'What led you to the property in Anglesey? Why there?'

'I got the impression it was random,' Harry lied, hoping he hadn't just contradicted Beth and Charlie. 'We drove all over the place.'

Goodman studied Harry for several long, uncomfortable seconds before scribbling something down. 'Let's continue, shall we? There's still a lot to get through and I'd like to open the discussion up to my colleagues.'

And so it went, backwards and forwards, analysing every moment of Harry's experience, from the crash on the peak to Vela's ship disappearing out to sea. And everything in between. Harry told them as much as he could while trying to protect Zhen and Dougie, and the farmhands, Colin and Ewan. He never mentioned Vaughn, other than that the heavies wanted to rough Beth up over money, but Goodman and his chums didn't seem interested in Lugers or Liverpudlians. All they cared about was Vela, and the missed opportunity he represented. He kept Beth and Charlie out of everything, taking every opportunity to profess their innocence.

He just wanted his family back. For their lives to return to normal.

How that would happen, he had absolutely no idea.

CARGO

Days passed.

The discussions were numerous and intense, as were the transatlantic phone conferences. None of them involved Nash, but he considered himself privileged to be a part of such an incredible event. Eventually, decisions were made and orders issued. Now it was just an exercise in logistics.

So they gathered for the last time inside the giant hangar. Goodman and his Condor colleagues, Nash, Chambers and Phelan, Hughes and his soldiers, and Fisk, all standing a short distance from the craft. Once again it had been shrouded, this time in thick black plastic sheeting, and reloaded onto the Antar's trailer. Prior to that, it had rested on a steel frame, a small staircase braced against the only accessible hatch.

Over a period of several days, a small, specially selected team of people had inspected the inside of the craft. Despite their earlier, unauthorised incursions, Nash and Chambers had no trouble expressing their sheer wonder at what they saw. After the Condor group had enjoyed their fill, a succession of British boffins had crawled all over the interior with a myriad of equipment. Nash and his team had supervised them and witnessed their frustrated endeavours. Besides the cockpit, the only other area they could gain access to was a small ante-room, where a section of twisted bulkhead had created a gap just big enough to see through. The room beyond was blank and featureless, and the boffins had wanted to use cutting gear and jackhammers to break in, but it was Fisk who called a halt to the British efforts.

No one argued, not even Goodman and his Condors. After all, Fisk was a representative of the shadowy and infinitely more powerful Majestic Twelve group of politicians, scientists and military figures that, unlike most of the world, Nash knew existed. It was Fisk who'd controlled access to the craft, Fisk who'd arranged for the alien bodies to be frozen and flown off the base, and Fisk who'd ordered Dougie Booth's corpse to be dumped at sea.

A phone call from Fisk had also summoned a mighty US Navy transport vessel to the port of Cambeltown just three miles away, and it was Fisk who would escort the craft back across the Atlantic Ocean, who would oversee the journey to its final destination somewhere in the United States. Maybe one day Nash would find out where that was. Maybe.

The Condor group was first to leave, congratulating Nash and his team on a job well done before being whisked away in a fleet of powerful saloons. Hughes and his men left too, tasked with overseeing physical security for the short trip to the docks. Nash took a final walk around the craft, ostensibly to check the straps and lashings, when in fact he was taking a last look, to touch it one final time, to marvel at its journey across the galaxy. He circled the craft, draped in its funeral shrouds, its shape purposely distorted by timber frames and mundane signage, and Nash experienced a twinge of sadness. She was like a once-proud ocean liner, about to embark on its final journey to a ship's graveyard, where she would be bent, twisted and sliced open by an ignorant race of primitive beings. The mental image made him feel a little ashamed.

Nash finished his circumnavigation and stood next to Fisk. 'So, what will happen to her?'

'We're gonna clean her up real good, then charge Joe Public five bucks a piece to look inside. They'll be lined up around the block for decades.'

Nash gave the American a sideways glance. 'Funny.' Yet he could see Fisk was deciding how much he could tell them. Not much, Nash guessed. The special relationship only went so far.

'This isn't our first rodeo,' the American told him. 'We've dismantled two other craft, put things under the microscope, tried to figure out exactly what we're looking at and how it ticks. The best minds in America are working night and day to unlock the secrets of recovered technology, but the truth is we're cavemen standing around a telephone and wondering how the damn thing works.' Fisk shrugged and said, 'It's a challenge, but one day someone will crack the code. I just hope I'm still a part of this when we do.'

'Me too,' Nash echoed.

Fisk checked his watch. 'It'll be dark in thirty minutes. Have Stone and his buddy ready to roll on the hour.'

'The road is being cleared as we speak. It'll be a straight run to the dock.'

'There'll be no cross-loading,' Fisk warned. 'The whole rig goes onto the ship. Then it's *adios*.'

Nash thrust his hands in his pockets. 'Well, it's been a

pleasure working with you, Joe. Maybe we'll work with each other again.'

'Who knows? It's a small world.'

Nash turned back to the craft, still marvelling at its very existence.

'Feels even smaller now.'

HARRY, Beth and Charlie remained at RAF Machrihanish for another ten days, which turned out to be a reasonably pleasant experience. They were given their own house, a vacant family unit at the edge of the base, and Charlie spent his time reading and taking walks with his parents. He seemed unfazed by everything that had happened, and once again Beth and Harry were struck by their son's growing confidence. For now, Charlie appeared to be the winner in all of this. Harry and Beth prayed that would continue.

They'd been re-interviewed several times since they'd first arrived, always by Goodman and his two nameless colleagues. Harry was sure Goodman wasn't his real name, but it didn't matter. All that mattered now was getting home and rebuilding their lives.

They'd undergone further tests and physical examinations, and the doctors seemed interested in Charlie's ability to withstand the telepathy he'd experienced, but they failed to find anything troubling. They hadn't known Charlie beforehand, and neither Harry nor Beth elaborated on their son's mental and emotional improvements. They wouldn't give anyone a reason to put their son under a microscope.

The interviews ceased after a week, and they were left alone. They went for long walks around the base perimeter, always shadowed by an unarmed RAF soldier, and Charlie had enjoyed watching the planes come and go. A gilded cage it might be, but it was still a cage, and every night after supper Harry and Beth lay in the dark of their bedroom and spoke quietly about what lay ahead. Nash had allowed a single phone call, and they'd discovered that Dougie had gone missing. Rita had been inconsolable, and Harry had made arrangements with a couple of local farmers to keep things ticking over. But it wasn't enough. They had to be there.

After ten days a jeep pulled up outside their house and a grizzled sergeant told them they were leaving. It took them less than fifteen minutes to pack and vacate the property, and the sergeant drove them to a single-storey brick building near the main gate. Harry was pleased to see it had windows, albeit covered with rusted steel mesh, but nonetheless it was a novel experience to be summoned to a room that didn't feel like it was deep underground.

Nash waited for them in a small office with runway safety posters on the walls. It was the first time Harry had seen him in over a week, and he rose from behind a desk when they entered, inviting them both to sit in the chairs opposite. Charlie remained outside, chaperoned by the driver. Nash closed the door and retook his seat.

'You'll be pleased to know that our investigations are now complete and you're free to leave. There's an aircraft waiting to take you back to Oswestry. Your Land Rover was recovered from Anglesey and is waiting at a local airfield.' Nash took two sheets of paper from a drawer and slid them across the desk. 'I need you to sign these. Both of you.'

Harry picked his up and studied it. There was a government seal at the top, and the body of the text was littered with legalese that spoke of national security and confidentiality.

'I've already signed the official secrets act, back when I was in uniform.'

'The world has changed since then, Harry.'

'Sign it,' Beth told her husband, in a voice that dared him to argue.

Harry didn't. The papers were signed and Nash put them back in the drawer.

'You're not to discuss these matters with anyone. Anyone,' Nash repeated. 'I can't stress that strongly enough.'

'What about our friends, my family back in Ilkeston? People have been worried—'

'You're not to talk about this, Missus Wakefield. That's final.'

'The villagers, they'll ask questions. What do we tell them?'

'You tell them nothing.'

'But we—'

Harry squeezed Beth's hand. 'That's enough, love.' He looked at Nash and said, 'If we talk, bad things will happen. Right, Mister Nash?'

Nash stared back at him. 'I don't make the rules.'

'We just want to get on with our lives,' Beth assured him.

Nash studied them for a moment, then he pointed to the meshed window. 'The fact is, the world is not ready to accept what you and I know to be true. That we are not alone in this universe. That God's creatures take on many forms and inhabit countless planets across the galaxy. And while we might think of ourselves as an advanced species, we are but savages compared to those who operate craft like the one that crashed on Craggan Peak. Not everyone can accept such things. To be frank, I sometimes struggle myself, but imagine the chaos and hysteria that would ensue were that knowledge made public.'

Harry understood. So did Beth. 'We won't say a word,' Harry assured him. 'We just want to go home, forget this ever happened. Start again.'

'Good.' Nash got to his feet. 'The driver will take you to the aircraft.'

Harry and Beth stood. 'What happens when we get home?' he asked. 'Legally, I mean. I wounded two men with an unregistered gun. How do I explain that to the police?'

'You don't,' Nash told him. 'The police have no interest in you, and all criminal matters pertaining to the events of the last few days have been expunged from any records. You're both free to carry on with your lives.'

'Are you sure?' Beth asked, her voice trembling with relief.

'No one will give you any trouble,' Nash told her. 'That works in our interests too.' He opened the door and Charlie smiled at them. Nash handed Harry a business card. 'We'll be in touch from time to time. If there's anything you need to tell me, anything you've forgotten, you have my number.'

Harry took the card and turned it over. There was an Air Ministry logo on one side and a phone number on the other: *Whitehall, 1100*. Nash shook Harry's hand.

'Until we meet again.'

'Perhaps this is it,' Harry told him. 'Perhaps this is the end of this whole crazy saga.'

Nash gave Harry a wink. 'Now that would be disappointing, wouldn't it?'

They were driven out to the runway where the de Havilland waited. They climbed aboard and strapped in, and a few minutes later the plane was hurtling along the runway and lifting off. It banked out over the sea, and Harry turned and looked over his shoulder. He wondered what had become of the craft, the bodies, and he wondered where Vela was at that moment.

Millions of miles away, he reckoned. *Maybe billions.*

And like Nash, Harry realised that he didn't want it to end.

HOMECOMING

Under a bright winter sun, the aircraft touched down at Rednal airfield and taxied towards an empty apron. As soon as Harry, Beth and Charlie had disembarked, the de Havilland headed back towards the runway and took off again, banking to the west. *To the RAF base on Anglesey,* Harry guessed, and he wondered what had happened to Zhen. He hadn't seen him since the cell door had closed behind him, and neither Goodman nor Nash had elaborated on his status, other than to assure Harry he was in good health. He was already thinking about taking a trip to the island, not only to reassure himself that things were okay but also to revisit the scene of Vela's departure, a wondrous event that continued to fascinate him.

A waiting airfield worker in oily overalls handed over the keys to the Land Rover and marched away. Harry saw that the vehicle had been cleaned and refuelled, but he imagined it hadn't been done out of courtesy. More likely someone had crawled all over it with a fine-tooth comb.

They drove west, back towards the mountains and home. Snow had fallen in their absence, and it blanketed

the hills in white. The rooftops of Finnhagel were topped
with powdery crowns, and as Harry steered the Rover up
through the village, a few locals stopped and stared. Some
waved, but it was a tentative gesture. Almost reluctant,
Harry felt. He wasn't expecting bunting and a brass band,
but he expected a little more enthusiasm than what was on
offer. He exchanged a look with Beth as they passed *The
Griffin,* and her frown told him she was equally bemused.
No one smiled either, and Harry's earlier optimism waned.

They left the village behind them and started climbing
the track. The first sign of trouble was when Dougie's
cottage rolled into view. At first Harry thought it was in
shadow, but as they drew nearer, he realised what had
happened.

'Oh no,' Beth gasped as Harry slowed down. The stone
walls of Dougie's cottage were blackened, the roof gone,
leaving behind a ribcage of blackened timbers and a house
exposed to the elements.

'Go, Harry! Quickly!'

Beth feared the worst as Harry put his foot down,
weaving up and around the hillside towards home.

Or what was left of it.

'Oh my God! No!' Beth gasped as they caught sight of
the house.

Not a house, Harry realised. 'Try to stay calm,' he
warned, mindful of Charlie sitting behind them. Beth bit
her lip, but the tears were already rolling down her face.

The house was gone, pretty much. Everything that
could burn was charred to nothing, every door, every
window, and the roof had caved in, not a partial collapse
like Dougie's, but completely, leaving nothing but a burned-
out shell.

'Stay there,' he told Beth, who held a confused Charlie

against her legs. 'I'll see if there's anything to be saved.'

'No! It's too dangerous,' Beth warned.

'I'll be in and out. Don't move.'

Harry's boots kicked up grey ash as he marched towards a front door that was no longer there. Beyond it was a black grotto of destruction. The hallway was gutted and stank of smoke and petrol. The snug was nothing more than a charred graveyard of sticks and what might've once been furniture. Fractured masonry and piles of bricks lay all around him. Every window had been blown out, every wall blackened. In the kitchen, the oil-fired cooker had made its own destructive contribution to the inferno. The stairs led up to spikes of scorched timber and a clear blue sky. Harry coughed as a sudden breeze whipped up clouds of soot and ash. He stumbled out into the garden, spluttering and rubbing his eyes.

Oh, God.

Every one of his outbuildings was gone, burned to the ground, leaving behind blackened brick pillars. Timber, feed, hay, all of it destroyed. Dead chickens littered the cobbles, necks wrung, feathers charred. Charlie's chickens. Then he saw something else, beyond the boundary wall. Indistinct shapes lying in the snow. Off-white shapes, marked with red. Harry used blue dye on his animals.

Slaughtered sheep.

'No,' he whispered.

Harry's anger boiled like lava. Despair squeezed his throat. He wanted to scream and rage, but not with Beth and Charlie around. He heard the whine of a Land Rover coming up the track. He ran around the house. Beth was still standing on the path. Charlie was holding her hand, looking bemused.

'Keep Charlie there!' he shouted at Beth. 'Don't let him wander.'

The Land Rover came to a halt on the track. Ewan and Colin climbed out, wrapped up in coats and boots, sombre faces beneath their hats. Harry led the boys away from his family. Only when they were well out of earshot did he let Ewan speak.

'Happened in the middle of the night, Mister Wakefield. Gavin says he saw a jeep driving back down through the village, going like the clappers. Didn't get a look at the driver though, and the number plate was covered in mud.'

'What about Dougie and Rita? Where are they?'

'No one's seen Dougie since that thing came down. Some say he's had a nervous breakdown.'

Tough-as-nails Dougie? Harry found it hard to believe. 'What about Rita?'

'She's in bits,' Ewan told him. 'Gone to her sister's in Wrexham.'

'Jesus, what a bloody mess,' Harry muttered, looking out over the hills.

'There's more,' Ewan said, and Harry could see by his face that something bad was coming. 'They set fire to the sheep pens as well, killed most of 'em. All the pigs too. The outbuildings are gone, and all the farm machinery had been sabotaged.' Ewan was close to tears. 'Who'd do such a thing, Mister Wakefield?'

Harry shrugged, but he knew. Beth probably knew too.

'Gavin says you can stay at *The Griffin* until you get on your feet.'

'Thanks, Ewan. That's something at least. I'll get Beth and Charlie settled in and then we'll see what we can salvage, eh?'

'Right you are, Mister Wakefield.'

197

As the boys headed back towards their jeep, Harry called after them. 'Colin, can I have a word?' He waited until Ewan was back in the Rover before he spoke. 'It's good to see you. How are you?'

The farmhand looked at Harry, a puzzled expression on his face. 'I'm fine.'

'Did they treat you okay?'

'Who?'

'The government people. In Scotland.'

Colin stared at him. 'Don't know what you're talking about.'

Harry stepped closer, kept his voice low. 'I know we're not supposed to talk, but I just wanted to make sure you're okay.'

'Talk about what?'

Harry frowned. 'I saw you at the airbase. We were there too, me, Beth and Charlie.'

Colin looked over at the burnt husk of Harry's farm. Finally he said, 'I've never been to Scotland, Mister Wakefield. You must have me confused with someone else.'

Harry opened his mouth to speak, then changed his mind. He could see the fear in Colin's eyes. Whatever he'd seen had deeply unsettled him, and Harry thought back to Nash's parting words, about the world not being ready for such things. At the time Harry wasn't sure, but as he watched Colin hurry away, he thought the man from the ministry was probably right.

He walked back to the house and took Beth in his arms. He held her tight as he watched Charlie walking along the wall of the opposite field, his arms spread like a high-wire walker. He seemed indifferent to the fact that his home had been destroyed, that his toys, his books and clothes were all gone. His life had been turned upside down, yet there he was, mucking about, chattering to himself. Harry didn't know whether to feel troubled or proud. He veered towards the latter.

'What are we going to do?' Beth asked, her head on his chest.

'We take Gavin up on his offer, get Charlie settled. As for the rest, I'll deal with it.'

Beth looked up at him. 'What d'you mean? We both know who did this. It was that Vaughn man. He's never going to let this go, is he?'

'No, he's not,' Harry echoed, the lava still bubbling. 'Let's get back to the village. We'll sort it out from there.'

HARRY UNLOADED their meagre belongings from the back of the Land Rover, just two small suitcases with a few clothes and toiletries. Everything they now owned had been given to them by the RAF. *History repeating itself,* Harry thought, remembering the day he'd reported for training at RAF Cardington with nothing more than the clothes he was wearing.

Gavin Souter waited at the back door, drying his hands on a tea towel. He slapped it over his shoulder and held out his hand as Harry approached.

'Good to see you again, Harry. You too, Beth.' He ruffled Charlie's hair. 'How's Master Charlie, then? In you go, young fella. Meg's in the kitchen. She's got ice cream.'

Charlie scampered off and Souter's smile melted. 'I know what they did up there. Bloody animals, I tell you.'

'Ewan said you saw them driving through the village.'

The landlord nodded gravely. 'I saw the light of the fires

first, then they came driving down the high street like the devil himself was chasing them. It was dark too, so I barely got a look at them. Thank God no one was in them houses.' He took the small suitcase from Beth's hand. 'Come on, let's get inside. I've got you in a nice room. And don't you go worrying about the bill either. We'll sort all that out when the time comes.'

Beth attempted a smile. 'Thanks, Gavin. That's very kind of you.'

They followed Souter into the bar. A couple of old-timers smiled and nodded. While Meg showed Beth and Charlie up to their room, Harry lingered in the bar. Souter poured them both a generous Scotch. He led Harry to the empty snug, and they took seats by the fire. Souter watched the door as he spoke.

'Those men you shot, they were villains, hard cases from Liverpool. What the bloody hell have you got yourself mixed up in, Harry?'

The fire crackled behind him, warming his back. At that moment, Harry felt he was never going to catch a break.

'They're friends of Norman's. Seems he'd run up a bit of a gambling debt, and Vaughn came to collect from us. Things got a little hairy up in the room and I had to shoot my way out.' Harry looked the landlord in the eye and said, 'I'm sorry, Gavin. I didn't mean to bring trouble to your door.'

Souter looked over his shoulder. When he turned back, he was smiling. 'People can't stop talking about it. I've had punters come all the way up from Oswestry just to see where it happened.' He shook his head. 'And that plane coming down, that ain't hurt neither.'

'Plane?'

'That's what they're telling us. Some experimental gizmo. Could be Russian too. All very hush-hush.'

'Not a spaceship then?'

Souter's nose wrinkled. 'Little green men? Don't be daft.' The smile slipped off his face. 'But while we're on the subject, someone came in the pub, while you were away. Clean-cut type, smart suit and hat. Never seen him before, but Meg was keen on him—then again, she's keen on most. Anyway, he chatted her up for a while, then he offered her money. For information.'

'About what?'

Souter leaned a little closer, his arms folded on the table. 'About you. Where you were. Where you might be hiding. With the space man.'

Harry swallowed. 'The what?'

'He had a picture with him, a kid's drawing, of a man with big eyes and a space suit.'

Charlie's drawing, Harry realised. Vaughn must've taken it after the shooting. Souter was still talking.

'The bloke was offering money to anyone who could give him information about the crash and the spaceman. Handed out copies of the drawing to a few of the regulars. He gave out business cards too, posh ones with fancy writing. Some folk said he was a reporter, but he was from Liverpool. One of Vaughn's people, probably.'

Harry recalled the drive up through the village, the blank faces, the half-smiles and reluctant waves. Harry and Beth were Johnny-come-lately's, not born and bred. That meant something in communities like Finnhagel. Their reappearance would set tongues wagging. Quiet conversations might be had, the lure of easy money too good to pass up. Eventually, someone would make the call.

Beth was right, this wasn't going to end anytime soon,

and when it did, it would end badly. Harry couldn't let that happen. He swallowed the rest of his drink and put his glass down.

'I need a favour, Gavin.'

The landlord raised an eyebrow. 'What's that, then?'

Harry held up his own business card. 'I need to make a call.'

COUNT ROOM

Jimmy Vaughn enjoyed watching the Sunday count.

He enjoyed seeing all that cash piled up on the table in neat stacks, liked to hear the chatter of his money-counting machine, the solid crunch of coin bags as they were loaded into the safe. And he liked to watch Max, his bookkeeper, beavering away behind his desk, his lightning-fast fingers punching keys and printing receipts, liked to watch him as he scratched numbers into two thick ledgers, the kosher one for the tax man, and the real one, with the real figures. Vaughn's ledger.

'How're we looking, Max?'

'Very healthy, Jimmy. It's been a good week.'

Vaughn had to agree. Yesterday's big win at Anfield had brought a few of the players in, and Vaughn had ordered the girls to make a fuss by massaging those oversized egos and encouraging ever-bigger bets. Easy money, Vaughn knew, and he made a mental note to slip an extra few quid into the girls' wage-packets next week.

The money was a means to an end, of course. Vaughn liked to spray it around occasionally, but what he craved more than anything else was an empire. Pubs and clubs were fine, and the boarding houses and caravan park turned a small profit, but they came with their own headaches. No, Vaughn wanted to branch out, go upmarket. The casino was his first, but he had plans for others. Restaurants too, fancy ones with unpronounceable menus and imported Frog chefs. And hotels.

There was a place down on Nelson Street, close to the station, that looked promising; twenty-five bedrooms, nice bar, a big dining room, old-fashioned entrance. Faded glory, the agent told him, and he was right. It was a dump, but a decent cash injection might turn its fortunes around. Put a sign up at Lime Street station, get the punters in, have a few working girls on standby for those lonely travelling sales-man. Good food, good service, good times. Yes, Vaughn decided, a hotel might be a very sound investment.

But it would need a chunk, and Vaughn wasn't keen on gambling his own money on the venture. He'd put in some, but the bulk of it would come from investors. *Greedy mugs,* as Vaughn liked to call them. There were plenty about. And debtors. A lot of people owed Jimmy Vaughn.

Like that couple in Wales, Fat Norman's family. The Wakefields. They were back from the dead and living in the pub, according to Terry. A couple of pig-eyed villagers had grassed them up, but no one knew where they'd been, only that they were back in circulation. Vaughn was intrigued. After Vic and Pat got shot, he'd sent men around the country to find the Wakefields, to stake out the homes of their nearest and dearest, but they'd gone to ground. Now they were back, but Vaughn had resisted the urge to drive down there and nail Harry Wakefield's hands to the wall. The debt had to be repaid, and that would help fund the hotel project, but Vaughn's mind kept drifting back to that space man Wakefield was hiding. He'd thought about it a lot, and he'd concluded that they'd stashed him somewhere, waiting for the dust to settle before springing him on the world as part of a lucrative newspaper and TV deal. The kind of deal that would buy Vaughn several hotels.

So the debt could wait. It was the space man that would cement his future.

But getting hold of him would require patience and planning. In hindsight, the arson was a mistake, ordered in a fit of rage. Now he needed to take a step back, be a bit more professional, have them watched, followed, like them spy films on the telly. *Patience is a bitter plant that bears sweet fruit,* he reminded himself. That was a good one. Max said that a lot. And Vaughn knew he was right.

So he'd let the Wakefields stew awhile. Not for long, but long enough to make them think that Jimmy Vaughn had lost interest and moved on.

'We're done,' Max said, breaking his chain of thought. The bookkeeper got to his feet and pulled on an overcoat. He handed Vaughn a stack of receipts held with paperclips. 'That's the breakdown, and the ledgers are both up-to-date. It's been a good week, Jimmy.'

'Nice work, Max.' Vaughn pocketed the receipts and clapped his hands. 'Right, everybody out.'

Max left the room, along with his cash-counters. A hulking heavy in a too-tight suit, hovered by the steel door.

'Go warm up the car, Brian. I won't be long.'

The heavy left, closing the steel door behind him. Vaughn threw the bolts, and then he started moving the cash from the table to the safe, stacking it into neat piles. This was one of his favourite jobs of the week. The cash-counters could do it, but Vaughn liked to get hands on, loved the feel of the notes in his hands, enjoyed stacking it in the safe in neat piles. Then he liked to stand back and admire it, because it symbolised all the years of hard graft, the sacrifice and bloodshed. Then he wondered how big a safe he'd need once he got his hands on that space man. *A much bigger one,* he decided. He was about to swing the door shut when he heard a tap on the steel door, followed by a muffled voice.

'Boss, it's Brian. There's a problem with the car.'

Vaughn tutted. 'Hang on, lad.'

He was still thinking about the money as he flipped open the door's security hatch, which was why he was unable to prevent the crowbar from jamming it open. Startled, Vaughn took a couple of steps back. Then he saw a hand come through the hatch. Holding a grenade.

'Unlock the door,' a voice ordered.

Not a Scouser, Vaughn realised. A posh lad. He hesitated.

'Unlock the door,' posh-boy repeated, 'or I pull the pin. I've got several of these, so unless you want the walls decorated with your intestines, I'd advise you to open up.'

Vaughn relented and threw the steel bolts. He always fancied his chances in a toe-to-toe, anyway. The door swung open. A man stepped over the threshold, a tall man with dark hair and hard eyes above a pencil-thin moustache. A man familiar with violence, just like him. There were others with him, six of them, and they were all dressed the same, polo necks and short overcoats. And they all carried guns. Automatics, too. Serious hardware.

'Who the fuck are you?' Vaughn demanded, standing his ground.

The hard eyes flicked to the safe. 'Empty it,' he ordered.

Vaughn watched his temple being desecrated as the neat stacks were toppled into several large holdalls. Notes fluttered to the carpet. Vaughn's blood began to boil. It wasn't the money itself, he could always make that back. No, it was the disrespect. Someone had sat down, hatched a plan, and was now stealing from Jimmy Vaughn in the mistaken belief they'd get away with it.

'Who are ya, lad?' Vaughn asked, his eyes watching the gun pointed at his belly. The bloke stood six feet away, one leg slightly in front of the other, his weight shifting every couple of seconds. Like a fighter, Vaughn realised, ready to defend the attack that Vaughn was contemplating. Probably not a good idea, he realised.

'At least tell me your name,' Vaughn pressed.

The man smiled, the gun never wavering. 'It's Nash. I'm a friend of Harry Wakefield.'

Vaughn raised an eyebrow. 'Is that right? Farmer boy's connected, is he? Seems I might've underestimated him. Who are you lads then? Birmingham mob? London?'

'We're more of a nationwide organisation,' Nash told him.

They emptied the safe, and Nash's men struggled outside with the bulging holdalls. Nash barked an order and two more hard-cases handcuffed Vaughn's hands behind his back.

'Hey, there's no need for this. You got what you came for.'

'Let's go,' Nash told him, waving the gun barrel.

Vaughn felt a shiver of warning. *Not just a robbery, then.* 'Go where?'

He felt strong hands on his shoulders and elbows, and they marched him outside and across the floor of the casino. Vaughn's mind raced. *Who the fuck was Harry Wakefield? Was that why Rolfe tried to rip him off in the first place?*

Because he knew people? And where the fuck were they going now?

His shoes scraped on the stairs, twisting down until they reached the lower basement. Cold air cut through his thin shirt as they pushed him into the underground car park. He saw his car waiting, lights on, engine running, boot open. He saw Brian inside, curled up like a baby, a ragged, bloody hole where his left eye used to be—

That's when Jimmy Vaughn knew it was all over.

There would be no beating, no interrogation, no torture, nothing like that. This was just business, pure and simple, and Vaughn felt the tension leave his body. He knew that someday it might end like this. It was all part of the game, and he'd never been frightened of dying, anyway. He'd had a good run too, done well for himself. He'd been someone, a face about town, a player. Not some fucking no-mark like the rest of the twats out there. Ma and pa would've been proud.

He watched his money being loaded into another idling saloon car, then Nash approached, and the men holding him tightened their grip. That's when the penny dropped. Vaughn's eyes widened.

'Wait a minute, I know you. You're that government bloke, the one who came into the pub that day, told everyone about the crash. It's you, isn't it?'

Nash tipped his head.

'What's this about?' Vaughn demanded.

'It's what we call overreach. You miscalculated.'

Vaughn's mind whirled. *Government men, with guns, here in Liverpool. Coming for him.* The reason didn't matter now. They'd discussed his name in the highest circles, his fate decided in a smoky, wood-lined room in some fancy London club. They'd deemed him a threat to the country, and for Jimmy Vaughn, that was a huge achievement. Like getting knighted, or something. Recognition. Respect.

He nodded at Brian's dead body. 'Not in the face, eh? I want an open coffin, so people can see me, pay their respects properly.'

Nash shook his head. 'There'll be no open coffin, because there won't be a body.'

The shiver became a tremble. Vaughn had buried lots of bodies, at sea, in other people's graves, in the foundations of buildings and flyovers. He never imagined he'd go like that himself, but then again it wasn't so bad, was it? *Jimmy Vaughn took his money, left the casino, and was never seen again.* It all added to the mystery. It'd keep people guessing, looking over their shoulder. And he'd be talked about for a long time, and that was important too. To be forgotten, well, that was the worst thing of all.

He watched Nash screw a silencer onto his gun, check it, then nod to the strong-arms. They bent Vaughn over the boot, shoved his head into Brian's belly. He felt the silencer touch the back of his neck.

'Tell me one thing,' he said, his voice muffled inside the boot. 'The space man, the flying saucer, it was all real, wasn't it, lad?'

'Every word,' he heard Nash say, and Jimmy Vaughn smiled for the last time.

'I knew it. I fucking knew—'

GUARDIAN

The weeks passed.

Winter sunk its teeth deeper into the Berwyn Mountains, but by March the snows had passed and the rains came, heralding the approaching spring. There would be no lambing for Harry and Beth, however. What animals had survived Vaughn's vicious revenge had been sold to other farmers, and life on Harry and Beth's farm was nothing more than a salvage operation. As a business it was worthless, and the supermarket contract had melted away like the winter snows. All they had left was the land itself.

The evening was a pleasant one, the weather calm and mild, and once again Harry drove up to the peak. He stamped through the ferns towards the crash site, or what remained of it. Mother Nature had colluded with Goodman and his people and buried the crash site under a deep blanket of snow, and the subsequent thaw had revealed little more than several bare strips of earth. Even the broken and twisted ferns had righted themselves, their dense ranks slowly reclaiming the muddy scars in their midst. Warm days and frequent rainfall would do the rest, and the incident on Craggan Peak would exist only in the memories of those who'd witnessed it. Harry considered himself lucky to be among their number.

As a pale sun dipped behind the mountains, Harry watched the first stars appear in the eastern sky, a reminder that his visits to the peak had become increasingly frustrating ones. He hoped he'd see something, on the ground or in the air, but nothing ever happened. Despite knowing the truth, the night sky had reverted to its former state of being, a magnificent, lifeless dome, and Harry missed the sheer wonder of past events. Nothing would ever feel the same again.

Beth had scolded him for his selfishness, reminding him that most people would go through life never being fortunate enough to see what they'd seen. Beth was right, as she often was, so the trips to the peak had become less frequent, and the hope that contact would once again be made, waned. As daylight faded across the peak, Harry took a last look at the sky then struck out towards the track.

He drove back down the mountain and considered the positives that Beth insisted he focus on. Charlie was one. His son had continued to improve, and the long periods of silence that had troubled Harry and Beth so much had shortened to the point of normality. His speech and vocabulary had improved significantly, much to the delight of his teacher, who'd insisted that it was the extra time she'd devoted to the boy that had tipped the balance. Harry and Beth knew better, but they allowed the lady to take credit, knowing the truth would never be believed. In any case, Charlie's contact with Vela had been a positive experience, and while he never really spoke about the visitor, occasionally he would see his son's eyes roam the sky. Just like his Dad's.

Another positive was Nash's phone call. Harry had taken it in Gavin's office, and Nash had explained that the Liverpool problem had been resolved and Harry was free to get on with his life. Harry had taken some convincing, and despite Nash's insistence, he continued to look over his shoulder, to watch for strange cars and listen for Scouse accents. It wasn't until someone had posted him a recent copy of the Liverpool Echo that he realised the threat had receded. One of the front page bylines read: *Notorious Liverpool businessman missing*. The article speculated that Vaughn had fled to South America in the face of a pending tax evasion charge, but Harry thought otherwise. Either way, Vaughn wasn't coming back, and the Wakefields could sleep a little more soundly.

But only a little, because the negatives in their lives far outweighed the positives. Dougie was still missing, and that troubled Harry a great deal. He'd vanished, and a devastated Rita had decided to stay in Wrexham with her sister. Harry and Beth had felt obligated to send her a little money to keep her head above water. Like them, Rita lost everything, including her husband, but the additional financial burden was a strain on their dwindling bank account.

The farm buildings had rotted unseen beneath a blanket of snow until the spring rains had revealed the devastation once more. Their solicitor was still negotiating with the insurance company over some detail or other, but no money was forthcoming, at least not yet. A distraught Beth had cursed her uncle in his grave and Harry didn't blame her. One way or another, he'd gambled away all of their futures.

Harry pulled the Rover off the track and parked outside the old house. With Ewan and Colin's help they'd cleared much of the rubble and torn down most of the charred timbers. Salvageable materials lay grouped around the courtyard, and Harry began stacking a few loose bricks into a pile. Of their home nothing much remained apart from stone walls and a couple of chimney stacks. It reminded Harry of an old Roman hillside fort, abandoned for centuries, weathered by time and the elements. A ruin in every sense. It was the same down at Dougie's place, and Harry wondered how they'd ever build it all up again. *If* was probably a better word.

He'd let Ewan and Colin go too, because there was no more work and no more money. They'd found jobs elsewhere though, and Harry got the impression Colin was glad to see the back of the mountain.

He heard a Rover winding up the track and saw Beth behind the wheel. She parked up and trudged towards him, the breeze plucking at her blonde hair. She wore a coat, boots, and a worried frown that Harry saw all too often these days. *More bad news.* He put down the bricks and slapped his hands clean. 'What's the matter?'

Beth folded her arms. 'The solicitor in Oswestry called the pub. He wants to talk to us.'

'What about?'

Beth shrugged. 'Whatever it is, it can't be good.'

'Maybe he's found a hidden pot of money in Norman's estate,' Harry quipped, but it was a wasted effort. He could see Beth was as troubled as he was.

'We're broke, we've nowhere to go, and we overstayed our welcome at *The Griffin* weeks ago. What are we going to do, Harry?'

Gavin had looked after them, but with no income, the Wakefields had become a drain on the pub's finances. The man had a business to run, and summer was just over the horizon. No one else in the village had offered them lodgings of any kind, and Harry thought that might be due to the lingering threat of the Liverpool gangsters. Nobody wanted *that* kind of trouble.

'When does he want to see us?'

'As soon as possible.'

Harry looked around the farm, a place he'd grown to love. Then he thought about packing up and leaving, going back to Ilkeston, staying at his mother-in-law's, sharing a room until they got on their feet. And Charlie, disrupted again, sent back to his old school, his progress threatened by big classes and small-minded bullies.

Yet they had no choice. They were out of options. Best to bite the bullet, try to start again.

'Let's go see him now. Might as well get it over with.'

They went back to the pub, washed and dressed in clean clothes, then drove down to Oswestry after lunch. They waited in the solicitors' outer office, Beth's hand clamped in Harry's as an unsmiling secretary tapped away at a typewriter. Eventually the frosted glass door behind her opened and the solicitor, a plump, balding man in a navy pinstripe, invited them into his inner sanctum. His name was Townsend and his office was neat and impressive, with dark wooden furniture and bookshelves crammed with legal volumes bound in green leather. Former partners captured in oils looked down from the white-painted walls. The room reeked of order and prosperity. About as far away from Harry and Beth's life as it could get.

Townsend pulled out chairs for them both and sat behind his neatly arranged desk. Harry glanced at the open file that lay there and glimpsed the documents inside; *Title Deeds* and *Land Registry*. Beth sat rigid in her chair.

Townsend cleared his throat and Harry sat a little straighter too. Steeling himself.

'Thank you for coming at such short notice,' Townsend began, his hands folded on the file in front of him. 'Did you manage to park okay? Market day is always busy here, what with the traffic and the visitors.'

Harry wasn't in the mood for small talk. 'I don't want to be rude, but we've got a lot on our plate at the moment and we'd really appreciate it if you got to the point.'

Beth gave Harry a disapproving glance. 'You must forgive my husband, Mister Townsend. He's been under a lot of strain lately. We all have.'

Townsend nodded gravely. 'The farm, yes. A terrible business. I don't suppose they've found the culprit yet?'

'No. And even if they did, they won't pay for the damage, will they?'

'Harry!' Beth protested, struggling to keep things civil. She gushed at Townsend. 'I'm so sorry, I don't know—'

'Stop apologising,' Harry snapped. He turned to Townsend and said, 'Look, just tell us why we're here. Put us out of our misery.'

Harry choked back the anger. He stared at Townsend, waiting for the verdict to be delivered, the words that would change their lives, that would banish them from the mountain to a future of handouts and favours. Until they got back on their feet. And that could be years away.

Townsend leaned forward, his elbows on the table, his fingers interlocked. He looked at them in turn, his brown knitted with concern. 'Well, I've finally received a reply from the insurance company. It's not good news, I'm afraid. It appears that Mister Rolfe was behind on his payments, which rendered the policy void.'

'But we've paid into that policy since we've been here,' Beth protested.

'Mister Rolfe scaled down the coverage.' He handed them a cheque. 'This is their final settlement.'

Harry took it and stared at the figure. 'This won't cover what we owe. Nowhere near it.'

'Insurance companies can be a law unto themselves,' Townsend muttered apologetically.

'So, what do we do now? What are our options?'

Townsend tapped the file in front of him. 'The land has some commercial value. Renting it to local farmers is an option, but that doesn't solve your accommodation problems.' He cleared his throat and said, 'My advice would be to sell. I've prepared the papers, should you decide to do so.'

Beth stifled a sob and rummaged for a handkerchief in her bag. Harry got to his feet. 'We'll sleep on it, if you don't mind. It's a lot to think about.'

'Of course,' Townsend nodded, standing. He held the door open, and they stepped out into the outer office. As they headed for the street, the secretary called after them.

'Mister Wakefield?'

She was holding out a letter. Harry took it from her. 'What's this?'

'Our invoice,' she told him. 'If you'd be kind enough to settle in thirty days, I'd be much obliged.'

THE DRIVE back to Finnhagel was a blur. Beth cried for most of the way, and Harry didn't want to think about what lay ahead, but at least they knew there was no money coming. It wasn't what they wanted to hear, but now the decision had been made for them. They were leaving the mountain, whether they liked it or not.

'We'll tell Gavin tonight, leave in the morning. No point in delaying the inevitable. You can give your Mum a ring from the pub, tell her we'll be there sometime tomorrow.'

'Fine,' Beth sniffed, dabbing her eyes with a handkerchief.

'You pick up Charlie from school. I'll drive back up to the farm, pick up the jerry cans, tools and some other bits, pack it all up.'

'What about the other Rover?'

'I'll give it to Gavin. It's not worth much anyway, but it'll help pay towards what we owe.'

'Good. It's the right thing to do,' Beth agreed.

Harry drove back to the farm and packed up everything worth taking, which wasn't much at all. He climbed back into the Rover and started the engine, but instead of heading down to the village, he swung the vehicle around and headed up towards the peak.

When he cleared the forest and parked by the side of the track, it irritated him to see other people already there. He watched them heading across the moorland towards him, a dozen brightly coloured rain slickers snaking their way through the ferns. Hill-walkers, Harry realised. Since the crash he'd treated the peak as hallowed ground, as if he had a personal connection with the soil beneath his feet, but he knew it was a childish attitude. The peak didn't belong to him, or anyone. It was there for all to enjoy. As it should be.

He sat there a little longer, looking out over the vast, gently sloping hillside that reached up to the jagged saddle above, until the hill-walkers were within shouting distance, and then Harry said a silent goodbye. Everything that had happened here was in the past. What lay ahead was uncertain.

He drove back to *The Griffin*. Beth and Charlie were in

the room, and Harry spent some time with his son, hearing about his day in school. Charlie jabbered excitedly, and Harry shared a look with his wife; neither he nor Beth had the courage to tell him he wouldn't be going back.

'You mustn't be sad,' Charlie said, as he tackled his homework at the small writing table.

Harry was lying on the bed, reading a newspaper. 'Sad about what?'

'It'll be okay.'

Beth frowned. 'Of course it will, darling.'

Charlie turned around in his chair and smiled. 'I knew he'd come back. He told me he would.'

Harry frowned. Beth looked puzzled. Harry opened his mouth to speak, but the knock at the door cut him off. Gavin was waiting outside.

'Sorry to disturb, but you've got a visitor.'

'Who?'

Gavin lowered his voice. 'A Chinaman. He's downstairs in the snug. Odd little fella.'

Harry and Beth turned and looked at Charlie. The boy smiled. 'See?'

And that's where they found Zhen a couple of minutes later, sitting at a large table by the fire, reading the *Daily Express*. A jumper and corduroy trousers had replaced the oriental clothes. He got to his feet when he saw them and offered a small bow.

'Mister and Missus Wakefield. So good to see you.'

'You too,' Harry told him as they shook hands, and Harry meant it.

Zhen laid a gentle hand on Charlie's head. 'How is Mister Charlie?'

'Okay,' Charlie grinned.

Harry ordered tea and sandwiches, and they

waited patiently as Meg fussed back and forth with pots and trays. Then sipped their brews as the fire crackled and spat in the grate. It was Harry who broke the silence, setting down his cup and clearing his throat.

'What happened to you? In Scotland?'

Zhen shrugged. 'They asked questions. I gave them answers they didn't believe, which angered them. Now they have ordered me to leave the country.' Zhen smiled. 'This pleases me, however. Many years have passed since I've been home.'

'Where's home?' Beth asked him.

'Tianchizhen, in China. It's a small town near the Mongolian border. Or was, when I left.'

'When were you last there?'

'Eighteen-oh-seven.'

Beth cocked her head. 'I think you mean nineteen-oh-seven.'

'Eighteen-oh-seven,' Zhen repeated, smiling.

Harry did the math. 'That's a hundred-and-fifty-six years ago.'

'Earth years, yes.' He pointed to the ceiling. 'I have travelled aboard the Explorers' ships many times. It changes things.'

Harry's jaw dropped. 'You've *what?*'

'It is how they can cross the galaxy, by bending space and time. A day of travel can often mean the passage of several years here on Earth, however, I do not try to make sense of these things, I only accept them.' He smiled, remembering. 'On one such journey, I returned to Earth on the day before I left.'

'That's not possible,' Harry whispered.

Zhen shrugged. 'Sixty years ago mankind was barely

able to fly. Now he orbits the earth in rocket ships. Who can say what is and what is not possible?'

Harry could barely believe it. 'You've *flown* in those ships?'

'As have you,' Zhen told him.

The fall. 'I don't know if—'

'Yes, you do. How else could they have saved you?' He reached into a leather valise by his feet and produced a stiff brown envelope. 'So, you are wondering why I am here, yes? Then wonder no more.' He extracted a sheet of paper and laid it on the table. 'As you can see, the relevant parties have already signed.' Zhen offered Harry a pen. 'All that is required are your signatures.'

The paper was thick and creamy, the legalese typed in neat, even blocks. Zhen's signature was there, alongside his name. 'What's this?'

'A transfer of title. If you sign it, you will become the new owners of Carmel Hall.'

'The manor house?'

Zhen nodded. 'The gateway needs new guardians, to protect it, to ensure its privacy. From time to time the Explorers will return, to continue their work, their quest for knowledge. This is a great honour, yet also a great responsibility.' He studied their faces for a moment. 'You are free to take a different path should you so wish. Although the boy would be most disappointed, I think.'

Charlie pleaded with his large brown eyes. 'We'll go, won't we Mum? Dad?'

'I don't know,' Harry said truthfully. This was all going so fast. 'Are you saying that if we sign this, we'll own that manor house? The land? Everything?'

'These things are immaterial. The gateway is critical.'

Harry winced. 'That came out wrong. I meant—well,

we're homeless, pretty much.' He felt Beth's hand squeeze his own. He studied her face, her eyes, and saw the answer right there. Any hesitation melted away. 'We'd be honoured.'

Harry and Beth signed the page. Zhen slipped it back inside the envelope and handed it to them. 'There's a business card inside, a solicitor on Anglesey. He will formalise matters.' He rose slowly to his feet, bones cracking, and tugged on an overcoat. 'Now, I have a boat to catch.' He pressed a trilby hat over his head and held out his hand. Harry took it.

'I don't know what to say.'

'Say nothing. Protect the gateway, that is all.'

Zhen turned to Beth and shook her hand. 'The boy is special, destined for great things. Take good care of him. Of each other.'

The tears rolled down her face. 'We will.' She gave him a gentle peck on the cheek. 'Thank you, Zhen. For everything.'

The Chinaman grinned. 'It is not me you should thank. They have chosen well.' He picked up his valise, then held out his hand. 'Goodbye, Mister Charlie. It has been an honour to meet you.'

Charlie shook Zhen's outstretched hand. 'I knew you'd come back.'

The Chinaman bowed. 'Naturally.' He smiled one last time, turned on his heel and hurried to the door. Moments later he was gone.

Harry dropped into his chair, winded. Beth sat opposite, scooping Charlie onto her lap. 'I can't believe it,' she muttered.

Harry shook his head. 'Me neither.'

Beth smoothed Charlie's hair, her mouth close to his

ear. 'I don't need anyone to tell me you're special, Charlie Wakefield. I knew it the moment you were born.'

Harry stared at his son. '*Destined for great things,* that's what he said. You heard him, right Beth?'

'I did.' She kissed the top of Charlie's head.

Harry picked up the envelope and ran his fingers around the edges. 'How much does it cost to run a manor house, d'you think? Heating, electricity, repairs, gardening. That place must've been at least ten acres.'

'I don't know. A lot.'

'How are we going to manage?'

'We'll find a way,' Beth told him. 'There's plenty of land. We'll grow some veg, maybe rear a few sheep, chickens. That could bring in a little money.' She ruffled Charlie's hair. 'You'd like some more chickens, wouldn't you, young man?'

'You can use the paper,' Charlie told her, pointing.

Beth frowned, her eyes flicking to Zhen's discarded copy of the *Daily Express*. 'Oh, he forgot it.'

Charlie shook his head. 'No, he didn't.'

Harry looked at his son, his eyes narrowing. There was something so definite about his words. 'What d'you mean, Charlie?'

'Zhen left it for you.'

Harry reached out and grabbed the paper. He unfolded it and spread it out on the table. His eyes travelled down the page, scanning the words, the images.

I returned to Earth on the day before I left...

Harry looked up at his wife. 'How much money do we have? In the bank account?'

'Not sure. I'm too frightened to check. Why?'

'We need to get down to Oswestry, draw it all out. There's a bookies in town, right?'

Beth paled. 'You want to gamble the last of our money? After everything that's happened?'

Harry smiled. 'This is different, Beth.'

'How?'

He held up the newspaper, his smile wide, his finger pointing to the top of the page.

'Because this is next week's newspaper...'

EPILOGUE

THE DRY DESERT wind picked up a little, the sand drifting across the dirt road that wound its way through barren hills. Fisk glanced at the jeep's mirrors as he monitored the convoy behind him, much of it obscured by the dust they were kicking up. He glimpsed the craft, still shrouded on the back of the Antar's trailer, fading in and out of the yellow cloud.

Almost home, baby.

A couple of miles ahead, the Groom Lake base shimmered in the rising heat. The Nevada Test Range facility was about as remote as it could get, a top-secret airbase hidden deep in the desert and surrounded by rugged mountain ranges that stretched for tens of miles in all directions. The climate was perfect for flight operations, and the layers of covert and overt security were the tightest Fisk had ever experienced, which made Groom Lake the perfect location for Majestic Twelve's interplanetary operations.

He kept his speed to a steady twenty miles per hour, shadowing the huge runway that was still undergoing further expansion. It had been a long journey, from the west coast of Scotland and across the white-capped violence of the Atlantic Ocean to the calm blue waters of the Caribbean Sea. There, the forty-two thousand tonne USNS *Big Horn,* a roll-on roll-off vehicle transporter ship of the US Navy's Military Sea Transportation Service, transited the Panama Canal before turning into the sea lanes that would take her north to the naval base at San Diego.

Docking after sunset, the Antar and its extra-terrestrial cargo linked up with a small but heavily armed security convoy and drove through the night to reach the gate at Amargosa Valley, just as the sun climbed above the eastern horizon.

Fisk had finally relaxed as they'd passed through the checkpoint and onto Department of Defence property, but it was still a seventy-mile drive to the base at Groom Lake. Seventy miles of empty, mountainous terrain, watched by a multitude of human and electronic eyes, both seen and unseen. *And maybe others,* Fisk pondered, as the road ahead forked away from the main Groom Lake facility and headed towards the low mountain range that formed the western edge of the base.

Fisk drove south for ten miles on another dirt road until the main base had slipped behind the mountain range and the convoy rumbled through a steep-sided valley. The turn wasn't signposted but Fisk knew it well enough, steering the jeep left onto another hard-packed route that headed straight towards the mountain. Ahead, gaping steel blast doors drew them in like plankton sucked into the mouth of a whale. Beyond the doors, a dark void. They'd finally arrived at their destination; S-4, the Papoose Lake facility that was without exception *the* most secretive installation in the United States.

The interior of the mountain was cool and dark, and

Fisk flicked on his lights as they drove across the concrete floor. They'd been hollowing out the mountain range since the Roswell incident in forty-seven, creating a base-within-a-base that orbiting Soviet satellites could not penetrate and politicians from Washington would never see, a series of nine hangars constructed beneath Papoose Mountain each the size of a football stadium, and all of them connected by nuclear blast-proof doors sixty-five feet high.

Leaving the security detail behind, Fisk's jeep and the trailing Antar drove through the first hangar and into the next, now brightly lit and marshalled by armed military police who waved them through a succession of open blast doors all the way into Hangar Seven.

And it was there that Fisk's twelve thousand-mile journey finally ended.

A small reception party waited, most of them Majestic personnel, the generals and admirals from a variety of defence and intelligence bodies, the scientific experts in propulsion, engineering and astrophysics. The medics were not in attendance because the bodies had been flown in weeks ago and now lay in the morgue several levels beneath Fisk's feet.

Motors roared and chains rattled as an overhead winch lifted the craft off the Antar and set it down on a specially constructed plinth. The tarpaulins were removed and CIA personnel with fire hoses washed down the exterior of the craft, the weeks of accumulated dirt, dust and salt running into the drains beneath its wide body. Now it stood black and gleaming beneath the grid of bright overhead lights, water dripping from the craft's body.

Fisk saw Brigadier-General LeRoy Cavitt approaching him. Cavitt had been involved from the very beginning, and had recruited Fisk from his role as an intelligence officer at the 509th Bomb Group, Roswell Army Air Field, shortly afterwards. The general was wearing olive utilities and a peaked cap, and he smiled as he held out his hand.

'How ya doing, Joe?'

'Tired,' Fisk told him. 'That was some trip.'

'Outstanding work.' He turned and admired the slick, black craft that now occupied Hangar Seven. Hangar's Eight and Nine were already occupied with the remnants of the Roswell and San Agustin crashes, and lay unseen behind closed blast doors, and Fisk wondered if all the hangars would ever be filled.

'How were the Brits?'

'Learning fast.'

'Any fallout?'

Fisk shrugged. 'Limited. It was an isolated community, and they pretty much bought the whole *experimental craft* story. Time and disinformation will do the rest.' Fisk turned to Cavitt. 'The Wakefield guy was interesting though. Did you read the transcript?'

'The guy who jumped from the plane? Someone to monitor, for sure.'

'How about those life-supporting planets? *Millions* of them, Wakefield said. In our own galaxy.'

'Makes sense.' Cavitt pointed to the sealed blast-doors of Hangar Eight. 'Roswell was a different craft, different species. What does that mean? And why are they both here at relatively the same time?'

Fisk watched the other Majestic personnel circling the craft a short distance away, chatting, pointing, making notes on clipboards. 'What d'you think it means, sir?'

Cavitt folded his arms, took a deep breath and sighed. 'Christ knows. Their technology makes a mockery of ours and they come and go as they please. Maybe they're gearing up for something, invasion, colonisation, resource harvesting. One thing's for sure, they're not offering the hand of friendship, at least not yet. And now that we're dismantling their hardware and chopping up their dead friends, who knows what they're thinking.'

Fisk watched two transport trucks drive across the hangar and stop near the craft. The tailgates were lowered and several troops began to unload tables and equipment from the cargo bays. The noise echoed around the vast cavern.

'I got another job for you, Joe.'

Fisk plucked a pen and notepad from his pocket. Beneath the peak of his cap, Cavitt's dark eyes were troubled.

'We have a problem in the Oval Office. Kennedy won't let this thing go. He's been pressuring McCone at Langley for months, and now he's talking about disbanding Majestic.'

'Is he serious?' Fisk asked, incredulous. 'He's a former intel officer, for chrissakes. He should know better.'

'You know what these Irish kids are like. Tenacious bastards. He's like a dog with a goddam bone.'

Fisk's pen hovered over his notepad. 'What is it you need me to do?'

'I need you to get a team together, shooters, the best you can find. They should be unmarried, no dependents, guys who'll do as they're ordered, without hesitation.'

'I'll need authorisation, official cover,' Fisk said, scribbling.

'McCone will take care of that. He's set up a training base at White Sands. Hand-pick the assets yourself, Joe. Guys who can operate in small teams and under pressure. Guys who won't be missed,' he added.

'Roger that.' Fisk made another note. 'What's our time frame here?'

Cavitt shrugged. 'That depends on Kennedy. The civil rights thing has got him distracted but he won't let this go. He's talking to McCone about public disclosure, and that can't happen. Ever. So you need to be ready, asap.'

'It'll take time. A couple of months at least.'

'Work fast, Joe.'

Fisk made a couple more notes, then shook hands with Cavitt and walked to his jeep. Back behind the wheel, he watched the equipment being moved into position around the craft, the portable lights being set up, the temporary hatch being carefully removed from the side of the craft. It was truly a thing of beauty, and Fisk wanted to stay, to watch and listen as the experts strategised on the dismantling procedure, as they discussed the exotic technology, but none of that was in his purview. In any case, he was pretty certain there'd be other opportunities to get up close and personal.

Whoever was visiting planet Earth, wherever they were from, they wouldn't stop anytime soon. Fast-moving, intelligently controlled machines were regularly criss-crossing the skies, and there wasn't a goddam thing humanity could do about it. Maybe Cavitt was right, maybe the entities were planning something aggressive, something global. If that was the case, taking out the President wouldn't make any difference at all.

But orders were orders.

He fired up the jeep and drove away. Halfway across Hangar Six, he heard the huge doors rumbling closed behind him, then a deep, seismic *boom* as they locked together. Like a retired aircraft in a military museum, the machine from Craggan Peak had flown its last flight.

As Fisk left the mouth of the complex and emerged into the bright desert sunshine, the thought of that strange, beautiful craft now trapped like a caged bird inside a hollowed-out mountain made him feel a little sad. A little, but not too much.

Because the race that had built them were Columbus, and humanity the Indians, gathered on the beach, staring in awe at the ships that had sailed over an unfathomable horizon, watching the explorers wade ashore in strange clothes and menacing armour, not knowing what was coming next. A bolt of silk or the blade of a sword. Fisk wondered what would happen when the entities finally engaged with mankind. Would it be the beginning of the end or the Great Leap Forward? He prayed it would be the latter, but only time would answer that particular question.

Joe Fisk put his foot down, the jeep kicking up a cloud of dust in its wake as he headed towards the Groom Lake facility that lay beyond the desolate mountain range.

HAVE YOUR SAY

Did you enjoy ***UFO Down***?

I hope you did.

If you could spare a moment to rate the book on Amazon, or leave a review, I would be very much obliged.

Many thanks for your time.

UFO DOWN

A TRUE STORY

At just after 8.30 pm, on Wednesday the 23rd of January 1974, hundreds of people in the Welsh villages of Corwen, Llandrillo and Llanderfel were rocked by at least one, possibly two, explosions, followed by a frightening earth tremor that lasted for several seconds. Furniture moved and buildings shook. Livestock and domestic animals shrieked and cowered in terror. Thousands of people saw lights streaking across the sky above the Berwyn Mountains.

Convinced that an aircraft had crashed, a local nurse set off for the mountains in her car, dreading what she might find. Once above the tree line, she stopped her vehicle, frightened by what she saw. High on the desolate mountainside was a large glowing sphere. Too far from the road to be reached on foot, all the nurse could do was watch. The sphere pulsed, changing colour from red to yellow to white. When she drove back to her village, a group of police and soldiers stopped her and ordered her off the mountain.

The official response was fast, with police and military units arriving within hours and sealing off the mountain roads. In the days that followed a larger military presence descended on the area. More roads were closed and farmers prevented from tending their animals. Military aircraft crisscrossed the skies and soldiers combed the mountainsides. They were hunting for something, but no explanation was ever given. Suspicious strangers roamed the villages, asking questions and taking photographs. They were never identified.

The incident was picked up by the media, with national TV and radio reports broadcast over several days. The Guardian, The Times and several other national newspapers gave the event in-depth coverage as did the Welsh regional and local press.

Speculation about the incident continued. An aircraft crash would have accounted for the noise, lights and keen official involvement. Witnesses describe seeing 'an Army vehicle coming down the mountain near Bala Lake with something large on the back of it', but the authorities refused to acknowledge anything unusual had taken place. Instead, they offered a variety of official explanations, including meteorites, shooting stars, torch-wielding hare poachers and wild imaginations.

In the months prior to the Berwyn Mountains Incident, the north of England had been plagued by an aerial phenomenon dubbed the 'phantom helicopter'. Over a hundred sightings were made of this object which was seen flying low at night, often over dangerous terrain and in appalling weather. These sightings largely took place between spring 1973 and spring 1974 and ceased immediately after the Berwyn Incident.

Despite the numerous sightings - which led to an official report that remains classified to this day - no explanation for the 'phantom helicopter' was ever found. However, something unidentified was certainly flying around the skies over the Berwyn Mountains during that period, and many of the witnesses remain convinced that it was looking for something.

Or someone.

THE LONG FALL

Flight Sergeant Nicholas Stephen Alkemade was an RAF rear gunner in an Avro Lancaster heavy bomber during World War 2.

On the night of 24 March 1944, 21-year-old Alkemade was one of seven crew members in an Avro Lancaster of 115 Squadron RAF. Returning from a three-hundred bomber raid on Berlin, Alkemade's aircraft was attacked by a German Ju-88 night-fighter, caught fire and began to spiral out of control. Because his parachute had gone up in flames, Alkemade jumped from the aircraft without it, preferring to die by impact rather than burn to death. He fell 18,000 feet to the ground below.

Miraculously, his fall was broken by pine trees and a soft snow cover on the ground. He was able to move his limbs and suffered only a sprained leg. The Lancaster crashed in flames, killing pilot Jack Newman and three other members of the crew. They are buried in the Hanover War Cemetery.

Alkemade was subsequently captured and interviewed by the Gestapo, who were initially suspicious of his claim to have fallen without a parachute until the wreckage of the aircraft was examined. He became a celebrated prisoner of war, before being repatriated in May 1945.

Alkemade worked in the chemical industry after the war. He appeared on the ITV series *Just Amazing!*, where former motorcycle racer Barry Sheene interviewed people who had, through accident or design, achieved feats of daring and survival.

Flight Sergeant Nicholas Stephen Alkemade died on 22 June 1987.

ALSO BY DC ALDEN

Invasion: Downfall

Invasion: The Lost Chapters

Invasion: Uprising

Invasion: Chronicles

The Horse at the Gates

The Angola Deception

Fortress

End Zone

The Deep State Trilogy

UFO Down

Never miss out on book news, bonus content, promo offers and new release discounts.

Visit the official website at:

www.dcalden.com

Printed in Great Britain
by Amazon

58074250R00147